THAT TIME I Kissed MY BROTHER'S Best Friend

A Time of Your Life Rom Com

JULIE CHRISTIANSON

Copyright © 2022 by Julie Christianson

All rights reserved.

No part of this book may be reproduced in any form or by any electronic or mechanical means, including information storage and retrieval systems, without written permission from the author, except for the use of brief quotations in a book review.

This is a work of fiction. Unless otherwise indicated, all the names, characters, businesses, places, events and incidents in this book are either the product of the author's imagination or used in a fictitious manner. Any resemblance to actual persons, living or dead, or actual events is purely coincidental.

*For Jack and Karly:
My favorite brother and sister combo forever!*

Contents

Chapter 1 — 1
Kasey

Chapter 2 — 14
Kasey

Chapter 3 — 26
Beau

Chapter 4 — 37
A Text Thread with the McCoys before The Ugly Sweater Dinner

Chapter 5 — 40
Elaine Graham's Christmas in July Holiday Schedule!

Chapter 6 — 41
Kasey

Chapter 7 — 51
Beau

Chapter 8 — 57
A Text Thread with the McCoy Cousins the Next Morning

Chapter 9 — 59
Kasey

Chapter 10 — 70
Beau

Chapter 11 — 77
Kasey

Chapter 12 — 86
Beau

Chapter 13 — 93
Kasey

Chapter 14 — 101
Beau

Chapter 15 — 107
Kasey

Chapter 16 — 118
Six Months Later — On Actual Christmas Eve

Chapter 17	120
Kasey	
Chapter 18	127
Beau	
19. Epilogue	138
One Year Later	
Acknowledgments	147
Also by Julie Christianson	149
About the Author	151

Chapter One

KASEY

"You're late for Christmas, Kasey." My mother announces this from the doorway of our turn-of-the-century Craftsman. She's wearing jingle bell earrings and a necklace made from miniature twinkle lights. "Daddy and I told you to be home yesterday."

Home is Abieville, a small town on a big lake in the Adirondacks. From our backyard you can see the water. If it weren't for all the trees, you could see the whole town.

"I got here as soon as I could," I say, and my still-motion-sick stomach lurches as the wheels of my suitcase bump up the last step of the porch. "I took the redeye from LAX, a connecting flight through Denver, then a ride share at the Albany airport so no one would have to pick me up."

"No *wonder* you look so terrible." She gathers me in for one of her famous hugs. And by *famous* I mean crushing. "Goodness, Kasey!" she shrieks. "Careful with my bulbs!"

"Sorry, Mom."

"Well." She wipes both hands down her Mrs. Claus apron. "The good news is I think I smoothed things over with everybody."

I wrinkle my nose. "About ... your bulbs?"

"Don't be silly."

"About the fact that I look so terrible?"

"No." She swats at a strand of red hair that's slipped from her bun. "About the fact that you were late for Christmas. We've been over this already."

My shoulders creep up, and I hazard a crooked smile. "But it's only July 1st, Mom."

She lifts a finger. "My point exactly!" She beams like she's a lawyer resting her case. "The whole family was expecting to decorate the cousin tree last night. You know that's Big Mama's favorite part of the holidays. And the only reason we're celebrating in July in the first place is to lift her spirits." She glances at the house next door and lowers her voice. "Well. Hers and Aunt Remy's."

"I really am sorry." My heart sinks like an anchor. "But you know I couldn't reschedule my interview." My mother stares at me, blinking. "For the job at *The Chronicle*? The one where I'd be the youngest person ever to lead one of their departments?" Another couple blinks tell me my mom still doesn't have a clue. "No big deal if you forgot," I say.

But it's kind of a big deal.

"Oh yes, that's right." She pats at her bun. "Your interview. At *The Chronicle*. Of course I remember you telling me."

Nope. Don't think you do. "Anyway, Ms. Witherspoon says she'll be making her decision by the end of the week, which is good because the rent in LA is killing me."

My mother clucks like a hen. Correction: like a hen in a Mrs. Claus apron. "If you need Daddy and me to help with—"

"No, thanks," I interrupt. "I can make it on my own. I just need a full-time salary, ASAP." I hoist my computer bag higher on my shoulder and adjust the grip on the handle of my suitcase. "Anyway, I'm all yours now. No distractions. Promise."

My mother nods at the battered computer bag. "Then why did you bring your work bag? It's not like you're a doctor on a house call."

Thanks for the reminder, Mom.

"I'm not planning to write," I say. "The laptop's just my little insurance policy."

Her eyes go wide. "Against what?"

"Not a what," I say. "A *whom*." And that whom is my brother, Brady. I peek past my mom into the house where Brady and I grew up. I haven't lived here since high school, but Brady moved back for a while after college. He finally got his own place down the street, but I still expect him to jump out and prank me. Again. "If Brady tries anything while I'm home, he'll end up in my next article. I can see the headline now: Brady Graham Breaks World Record for Worst Smelling Socks."

Cluck. "That's not funny, Kasey."

"Come on, Mom." I arch an eyebrow. "It's a little bit funny."

My mother's mouth twitches. "Brady forgot one pair of socks in his gym bag for a few months back in middle school," she says. "Is that a crime?"

"As the one who was in charge of laundry back then, I'm here to report the stink was basically a felony." I crane my neck, trying to see over her shoulder again. "Can I come in yet, or are we going to stand out here on the porch talking about Brady's feet?"

"You're right!" My mother throws up her hands. "Well, get on in here, then." She steps back to make room for me and almost knocks over a Yankee Candle on the console. It's eggnog scented, which is perfect for ninety degrees and eighty percent humidity.

I wipe my Doc Martens on the new doormat that reads KISS ME UNDER THE MISTLETOE.

"Kind of bossy for a welcome mat, don't you think?"

"Oh, Kasey. I think you're silly." She shuts the door and follows me into the front room. I'll admit, my insides ache. But the good kind. The very best kind. No matter how much time passes, this space still smells like home. Right now, it smells like our home at Christmas. Probably because of the giant Douglas fir in the corner.

There are no ornaments on the tree yet, but somebody's already strung it up with lights. Around the base is the Graham family's special Christmas tree skirt. It's made of forest green felt and trimmed with red satin ribbon. Plastic snowflakes run along the edge, except in the spots where our cat, Sprinkles, chewed them off a few years back.

My mother points at the bin labeled SPECIAL COUSIN ORNAMENTS and clucks again. She's really got the whole chicken thing down pat. "All four of the McCoy cousins were over here last night. And, of course. Mac brought little Daisy. But we couldn't trim the tree without you." She trades in the cluck for a *tsk tsk tsk*.

If you don't think there's a difference, you haven't met Elaine Graham.

"Darby and Olivia were *so* disappointed," she continues. "And Tess flat-out insisted on waiting for you to even open the box."

"They're all in their twenties, Mom."

"Mac is thirty."

"I stand corrected," I say, puffing out a laugh. "But I promise I'll make it up to all of them this week. I really do miss everyone so much."

My mother shakes her head and her jingle bell earrings. "What about me?"

"Of course I miss you, Mom."

I roll my suitcase next to the coffee table and set my computer bag beside it so I can drop onto our couch. Ah. Home sweet home. *Almost* sweet enough to forget the reason I haven't been back for five straight summers.

(Not a what. A *whom*.)

But internships at *The Chronicle* don't grow on trees, even the tall firs our town is named for. Dream jobs don't just land in your lap either. And I won't let anyone steal what I've been working toward. *Not this time.*

"Kasey Elizabeth Graham," my mother says. "Don't you dare put those boots up on that couch. There's a reason our upholstery's lasted this long. No thanks to you and your brother's feet."

Seriously? Are we back on Brady's feet again?

For the record, my parents have had the same oversized sectional since their wedding day. A matching armchair and ottoman sit across from it. All our furniture is thirty years old and also very beige. Mom likes to add pops of color to the decor with blankets she knits. And for extra flavor, she embroiders seasonal throw pillows. Right now, the ones on the armchair are red, white, and blue—I'm sure an homage to the 4th of July. But on the sectional, she's scattered nine pillows. One for every reindeer.

"Uh oh," I say, picking up the pillow closest to me. "I think you spelled Rudolph wrong."

She scoffs. "I most certainly did not."

"See?" I toss the pillow at her. "His name ends in a PH. Not an f. You can look it up if you want proof, but ..." My voice trails off.

"Humph." She examines the lettering, her nose right up to the fabric. "You might be right," she quips, peering over the pillow at me. "My daughter, the valedictorian." She sets down the pillow, and I stifle a smile. I really do love my mom. Sure, she's blustery and loud, but she also gives *interesting* hugs. And yes, she mentions I'm not a doctor—a lot—but I know she's proud of me, in her own way.

Her own *very special* Elaine Graham way.

"In any case," she says, "don't get too comfortable on that couch. Uncle Cubby brought over a pile of potatoes earlier, and they aren't going to peel themselves."

"No problem, Mom." I slip the rubber band from my too-tight ponytail, and my scalp begins to tingle. I kind of like the feeling to be honest. Self-torture must be a thing with me. "Can I shower first?" I ask. "The connecting flight to Albany was packed, and I don't feel—"

"I'm sorry, but there's simply no time, Kasey." *Tsk tsk tsk.* "And I'm not saying that's your fault—what with your being late and all—but *someone* needs to prep the potato salad for the 4th of July before we can start baking snickerdoodles for Santa. Oh! That reminds me. I really should pop next door to Big Mama's.

With Mac, Daisy, and the triplets all visiting, the house is pretty chaotic. I'm worried your Aunt Remy will forget she's in charge of getting the carrots to put out for the eight reindeer and …" Mom pauses and lifts one eyebrow. "Rudolph with a PH."

Ha! Told you I love her.

"You nailed it, Mom." I grin at her.

"Well, you got your smarts from me." Cluck. "Anyway, Auntie Mae will be here any minute. She volunteered to prep the ribs and corncobs for dinner since I'll be too busy hosting. And there's still so much to do! You know there will be at least sixteen of us for dinner." Her eyes bulge. "I hope we have enough corn!"

"It'll be fine, Mom. Take a deep breath. If it helps, I won't eat any corn myself until we're sure there's plenty for everyone."

She nods sincerely, like I just offered her a kidney. "Thank you so much, dear." She tilts her head. "Who needs a doctor for a daughter when you can have one who's so considerate about corn?" She runs her hands down her apron again. "We'll be eating at six o'clock sharp. Maybe set a timer so you won't be late." She glances at her watch, and our old-school phone rings in the kitchen. "My word! What's the emergency now? I can't ever get a moment's peace these days. I'll be right back, Kasey." She points at me. "Don't go anywhere."

I glance around the room. "Deal."

She bustles off, both arms whirling like branches in a hurricane. In the silence that follows, I lean back and finger-comb my long auburn curls. At least I washed and conditioned last night. I can still smell the coconut shampoo as I work through the tangles.

Not having time to shower isn't the worst thing that's happened to you in Abieville, Kasey.

But I shake off the thought as quickly as it comes. Feeling sorry for myself and wallowing in past humiliation isn't on this week's agenda. Only fireworks and mistletoe for Christmas in July.

On that note, I survey the living room. Mom has everything exactly the same as every other Christmas, almost like we're not throwing an extra one just to cheer up Big Mama and Aunt Remy. And even though it's too hot to roast logs on the fire, our stockings are still hung on the mantle with care.

Phil. Elaine. Brady. Kasey.

My grandmother, Josie Bradford—AKA Big Mama—knitted stockings for everyone in the family. First her four daughters, then all four of their husbands. When Mac was born—he's my oldest cousin—she started adding stockings for each grandchild. Ten in total. She offered to teach me once, but I turned her down. I was too worried I'd be terrible at it.

Perfectionism is a thief, and I sure let it rob me.

Around the rest of the room, Mom's put up all the decorations Brady and I made when we were kids. Cotton ball angels. Snowmen formed from ballet tights. Candy canes of clay painted white with thick red stripes. All my stuff is neater than Brady's, of course, a fact I used to pride myself on. But the truth is my brother probably had more fun making his. Even with coloring books and crayons, I always tried too hard to stay in the lines.

My stomach growls, so I dig a handful of green and red M&Ms from an angel-shaped dish on the coffee table. I'm picking out all the red ones to munch first when Sprinkles moseys around the corner. He looks at me, his tail swishing like he's on a parade float waving to a crowd. I make kissy noises to tempt him over, but he ignores me and climbs on top of the big box of cousin ornaments.

Someone must've hauled the box up from Big Mama's and Big Papa's basement. Probably Uncle Irv. He's the only one still willing to go down there on account of all the spiders.

Every year when we were kids, Big Papa would chop down a special tree just for his grandchildren. In the days leading up to Christmas, we'd trim the tree and have an Ugly Sweater Dinner. There would be egg nog and caroling around town. And each Christmas Eve, Big Mama gave us matching pajamas and new ornaments to open. We'd leave out snickerdoodles for Santa. Carrots for the reindeer.

Then we grew up.

Earlier this year, both Big Papa and Aunt Remy's husband—my Uncle Ted—passed away. My mom wanted to do something nice for Big Mama and Aunt Remy.

Something to heal their broken hearts.

So she and her other two sisters—my Auntie Mae and Auntie Ann—decided to revive the tradition of the cousins' Christmas tree. This, of course, required cousins. Half of the grandkids still live in Abieville, but the rest are spread across the country. A gazillion and one emails later, everyone agreed that those of us who had to travel would have an easier time coming home in the summer. And that's how this year's Christmas in July was born.

Mom had the original idea, so she's hosting the cousins' tree in her house. She hustles back into the front room now, both her arms still flapping. How she hasn't flown away by now is anybody's guess.

"Kasey!" She gasps, but at least she remains on the ground. "You're just sitting there?"

"You told me to wait for you."

"I did?" Cluck. "Well. That was Aunt Remy on the phone, and she *does* in fact have the carrots."

"Thank goodness." I wipe my brow in exaggerated relief, but Mom ignores my sarcasm.

"That's the good news." *Tsk.* "The bad news is Big Mama's got a stomach bug. She can't come for dinner tonight. She's going to rest up next door."

"Oh no," I groan. As crushing as my mother's hugs can be, that's how gentle Big Mama's are. I miss her sweet, soft smile and her glittery eyes. So much. "Should I go over there to see her?"

Mom waves me off. "Better wait until she's feeling up to it. I'm sure she'll be right as rain soon. In the meantime, Auntie Mae and I still need your help with the potato salad. Plus, you'll have to change before dinner. That outfit of yours doesn't qualify."

I check out my cut-off jeans, white t-shirt, and the plaid

flannel tied around my waist. Doc Martens aren't exactly formal, but my people aren't exactly fancy. "Qualify for what?"

My mother inhales, gathering all her patience along with all the air in the room. "For our Ugly Sweater Dinner, of course."

I snort. "We're not really wearing sweaters, are we? It's ninety degrees out."

"It's also tradition!"

"Yes. In December. For actual Christmas. When it's cold."

Her shoulders sink. "You don't have to remind anyone here that it's not really Christmas." She lowers herself onto the couch. She's basically a slump of mother beside me. "Everyone needs traditions, you know." She sniffles. "This year more than ever."

"Oh, Mom." My own nose begins to sting. "You're right. And I'm so sorry."

"It's all right." She slips a crumpled tissue from her apron pocket and dabs at her eyes. "You came home. That's what matters."

We're both quiet for a beat, then I meet her gaze. "How is Aunt Remy doing, anyway? And Mac and the girls? Are they all hanging in there after losing Uncle Ted?"

"As well as can be expected, I suppose." Mom sniffles again. "You know, most of the time Big Mama talks like Big Papa's just in the other room, and we don't correct her. But Aunt Remy's a whole other ball of wax. Not that she's actual wax. That would be strange." My mother pauses. Blinks. "She misses Uncle Ted like a fish would miss water. If the fish got thrown out of the bowl, that is." She gulps. "I swear if I lost your father ..."

"You won't." I lay a hand on her shoulder, hoping to comfort her and change this grim line of conversation. She and my dad adore each other. They have for their whole lives. Not to mention how *I* feel about my dad. He's my ally in the Graham family, and I can't go down this grim line of thinking. "Not for a long time."

My mother blinks. "God willing," she chokes out.

"Please don't cry," I say. "I promise to be a good sport for this whole week. I'll be the best sport ever. And I'll wear whatever you want me to, no matter how sweaty I get."

"Well, thank you, Kasey." She swipes at her eyes again, then stuffs the tissue back into her apron. "First the corn. Now this."

"There's just one problem," I say, with a wince. "I didn't pack an ugly sweater. I didn't even pack a cute one. All I brought are shorts, sundresses, and sandals."

"Oh, dear," she mutters. "This simply won't do, Kasey." When she starts fumbling for the tissue again, I scramble for a solution.

"The triplets!" I blurt.

She freezes. "What about the triplets?"

"You said the girls are staying next door with Aunt Remy and Big Mama, right? Well, Olivia has *great* fashion sense," I say. "Darby's *always* overly prepared. And Tess *loves* a good theme party. I'll bet one of them packed an extra sweater."

My mother nods, smoothing her apron. "You're right. They probably did." She unclogs her throat, then glances at the window like she can actually see them in the house next door. "You know, Aunt Remy sent me a picture of the sweater Mac's wearing to dinner," she says. "He's going to be stiff competition, because it's hands down the ugliest thing I've ever seen." Her mouth quirks—just a quick twitch—but my mother is coming back to herself. "There's an entire snowman glued to the front of it made of Styrofoam and felt and buttons. And the back side's got the snowman's ...umm ..."

"Backside?"

"Exactly!" She snorts, then covers her mouth. "Remy said little Daisy's been dressed like an elf since this morning. She's such a darling girl, and my word, has she ever grown since the last time they visited. What was she, two years old then?" She squints, calculating. "That horrible wife of his was here then, too, so it had to be before she took off with her Pilates instructor." My mother clucks and *tsks*. "Can you imagine? Leaving on her daughter's birthday? Such a shame." She lowers her voice. "And now Daisy's starting to look like her."

"Like Gwen?" I grimace. "That's got to be hard on Mac."

Mom shakes her head. "Don't get me wrong. That little girl is as cute as a button, with those big blue eyes of hers. And she's got these crooked little pigtails. I swear your cousin can't do Daisy's hair to save his life."

I chuckle. "Knowing Mac, that's hardly surprising."

"Oh, and just a heads up." Her voice goes low again and she frowns, like being quiet is a supreme effort. "Daisy doesn't talk."

"Really?" I tilt my head, trying to figure out her age. "How old is she now? Like five?"

"She will be in September. But it's not that the girl doesn't know *how* to speak. She just stopped. Won't say a single word to anyone." Mom puts a hand to her chest. "Not even to me. And I'm *very* easy to talk to."

"Oh, wow." I swallow a laugh. "That *is* hard to imagine." While I chew the inside of my cheek, my mother nods in agreement.

"According to Mac, Daisy clammed up right after Aunt Remy left Apple Valley and moved back here to Abieville. He thinks Daisy's silent treatment is the girl's way of showing everyone she's mad about her grandma leaving. Did you know Daisy calls Aunt Remy Little Mama? Like Big Mama. Except little."

"Yep." More cheek chewing from me. "I was able to Sherlock Holmes that connection myself."

"Hmm." She taps her chin. "I think of you more as a Watson," she says. "In any case, Daisy was here last night, and I've never seen a child stay so quiet for so long. When you were Daisy's age, you were always such a motor mouth. Talking, talking, talking. I must admit, on occasion, I was sorely tempted to wear earplugs." My mother pauses to gasp for breath.

Ah, the irony.

"You know what?" I pat her knee. "It's really good to be

home, Mom. And I'm sorry I was late. But mostly I'm sorry I was so annoying twenty years ago."

She raises an eyebrow. "Don't be silly, Kasey. You are *much* more annoying now." She starts snickering at her own joke.

"Good one, Mom."

"I *am* pretty funny, aren't I?" She bobs her head. "You know, you and Brady inherited that from me. Your father's got absolutely no sense of humor."

I glance around the room. "Where is Daddy, anyway?"

"Oh, he ran over to Auntie Ann and Uncle Irv's a while ago to pick up the butter. We need pounds and pounds of it."

I scrunch up my nose. "Why?"

"For the corn. And the potatoes. And the snickerdoodles, Kasey." She shrugs like I really should've Watsoned that out. "We've been storing our butter at their place, since they've got that giant refrigerator in their basement. And thank goodness they do, because what's a Christmas Eve without snickerdoodles for Santa?"

"A tragedy."

"Exactly!" She beams. "As soon as your father gets back from Auntie Ann's, you and I can get to baking those snickerdoodles."

"After we finish making the potato salad for the 4th of July?"

"Exactly!"

"While Auntie Mae is making ribs and corn for dinner?"

"Exact—" My mother cuts herself off, and her forehead crumples. "Now that you mention it, we might get a little tight in the kitchen. But we'll make do." She snaps her fingers. "By the way, I washed your apron."

"Ooh!" I sit up straighter. "The one with Nicolas Cage's face all over it?"

"Obviously. You're the one who wrote *KGA: Kasey Graham's Apron—Do Not Touch* across the middle in Sharpie." She chuckles again, then hauls herself up off the couch. "I'm going to pop over to check on Big Mama and get those carrots. You get your stuff put away and head to the kitchen."

"You know, I probably had time to shower."

"Too risky," she says. "Anyway, your old bed's fixed up with fresh sheets. And since your brother moved into his own place, that's one less person sharing the bathroom."

"Speaking of Brady, when will good old Smelly Socks be coming over? Is he at work today?"

"Oh, no. Dr. Swanson closed the pet hospital through the 4th of July, except in case of emergency. It'll open back up after the A-Fair." She claps her hands. "It just occurred to me you won't have to miss the A-Fair this summer!"

"Yeah, that's been *quite* the sacrifice." Around here, everyone calls Abieville's summer carnival the A-Fair. Some of the ladies at church balked at the nickname, but it's always stuck. Like the Ferris wheel half the time.

My mother heads toward the door. "Brady's been down at the lake all day hosing out the kayaks," she says. "Those things do collect a fair amount of leaves in the winter."

"I remember," I say with a smile. Christmas trees and kayaks? I'm starting to get into the double holiday spirit. "So, Mom. Are we allowed to wear our bathing suits at the lake? Or are ugly Christmas sweaters mandatory all week?"

She pauses at the door, like she's weighing the options. "I suppose either one would be okay." She taps her forehead. "As I recall, when Brady and Beau stopped by to say hi this morning, they were wearing swimsuits."

"Wait." My stomach heaves. "When *who* stopped by?"

"Brady and Beau." She meets my gaze and blinks. "Didn't I tell you? Beau Slater's back in town." My stomach plummets, like I'm falling off the Ferris wheel at the A-Fair.

Beau Slater? Back in town? In *this* town? Abieville?

My mother's lucky I don't throw up on her Rudolf pillow.

"You *so* didn't tell me, Mom."

KASEY

"Well, now you know, don't you?" My mother waves and chirps, "Toodles!" As she shuts the door behind her, all the blood rushes to my head. This is a nightmare. Worse than Freddie Krueger.

Beau Slater? How could he be here?

The guy is a big shot photojournalist traveling all around the world now. Not that I ever asked about him. Or looked him up on social media. Or paid attention to his whereabouts. Why would I do that? I can't stand him. Okay, I might have checked to be sure he was going to be far away this summer, taking very important pictures with his very expensive camera. All alone, by his very horrible self. So why is he in Abieville?

Oh no.

Either that's my heart pounding in my ears, or somebody is in our kitchen. My dad could be back from Auntie Ann's with the butter. Or maybe Auntie Mae showed up to cook the ribs and corn. Either one of them might've come in from the back porch. In Abieville, no one locks their doors. We don't even have fences in this town. Just backroads and lots of trees and a lake and—

The refrigerator slams shut. So does my throat.

What if Brady's the one in the kitchen? What if my brother

stopped by to let my mom know he finished washing out the kayaks? What if he brought Beau Slater with him?

I've got to get out of here. Faster than STAT. I dart my eyes to the stairs. The safety of my bedroom calls to me. I could just run up there now and camp out for the rest of the week. That wouldn't be weird, right?

Sorry, family. I flew all the way across the country so we could be together for the Bradford sisters' Christmas in July, but if you need me, you'll have to visit my room. I'm the one hiding under that Pottery Barn Jr. quilt I got for my thirteenth birthday. And yes, that's a One Direction poster taped to the ceiling. And a Nicolas Cage pillowcase on my bed. KGP: Kasey Graham's Pillow—Do not touch. Poke me once to say "I missed you." Twice for "You're a lunatic."

Totally normal, right? Yep, that's me. Totally. Normal. A kitchen cabinet opens and shuts.

Run, Kasey! Run!

Stumbling up the stairs, I pass the shrine of school pictures on the wall. The earliest ones are full of missing teeth and frizzy hair. Then came the braces and acne. After I discovered conditioner and Brady discovered weights, we got a few decent shots in high school. Finally, miraculously, the trail ends with our senior portraits. Brady first. Then me.

My brother, who's only eleven months older, graduated one year before me. As with everything else in life, I was stuck following him. I was also stuck in the same class as Beauregard Slater. If Abieville itself is small, our K-12 school is even smaller. There weren't *that* many kids to be friends with. So even though they were a year apart, Brady and Beau buddied up. BFFs. No sisters allowed. That's when my brother stopped playing video games with me. Then he stopped hanging around the house.

For the rest of our time under the same roof, Brady was either at golf meets or basketball games. Soccer or baseball practice. And Beau Slater was always with him, his best friend and teammate for every season. Have I mentioned how much I hate Beau yet? Okay.

Maybe hate's too strong a word. But I definitely feel for Beau Slater what anyone would feel toward someone who stole everything that mattered to her.

What exactly did he steal, you ask? First, as I've already mentioned, he stole my brother's attention. Maybe not literally, because attention wasn't something Brady loved giving me in the first place. But after Beau came on the scene, my brother's pranks really kicked into high gear.

I became the butt of all their jokes. Peanut butter on my bicycle seat. Purple hair dye in my shampoo. I never knew what fresh torment was on the horizon. So, yes. Beau Slater stole my brother *and* my ability to open my locker without a bullfrog jumping out. Then there were the really big things Beau figuratively stole.

Like my dreams.

Thanks to my dumb brother, Beau knew it was my goal to go to college and study journalism. He also knew that on the road to that goal, I desperately wanted to run our school's newspaper. He knew that when my interview with the paper's advisor was still three months away, I'd already started a countdown on my calendar. In Sharpie. I meant business.

But you know who went after the job of editor and got it over me? You guessed it. Benedict Beauregard. Don't worry, though. Two can play at that game. I got my revenge when I was picked to be in charge of our school's yearbook. I applied because *his* plan was to be a photographer.

Photographer with a ph.

You see where this is going, right?

Beau and I both ran for junior class president, and he won by three votes. The following year, I was named valedictorian. That meant I got to wear a special sash and give the speech at our graduation. How do you like them apples, Beau?

Since we had the same GPA and had taken all the same AP classes, Beau told everyone I got valedictorian because of favoritism from our principal. Our principal happened to be my Uncle Irv. Jerk. (Not Uncle Irv. Beau Slater.)

Either way, that favoritism was a lie. The truth? I'd taken extra classes at the community college, and that's why I got to be top of the class. It's also probably why I got into UCLA. Then I got an internship at *The Westside Chronicle*.

Now I'm about to get hired for my dream job, something Brady hasn't done before me. Something I've worked for my entire life. That's right. Once Ms. Witherspoon calls, the peanut butter and hair dye and bullfrogs will all be ancient history.

Except for one last insult to my injury.

You see, at the end of our graduation ceremony, after all our classmates had tossed their caps into the air, Beau came to find me. This wasn't hard because I was the only senior sorting through the pile of abandoned caps. They all looked the same. Green and shiny. That's why I'd put KGC inside the rim of mine in Sharpie.

Kasey Graham's Cap. Do Not Touch.

"Kasey!" Beau approached from behind, and I quickly straightened. My graduation gown was large and flowing like a shiny green tent. The shape wasn't flattering, but everyone had to wear the same ugly tent-gown. Even Beau.

"What do you want?" I swiped at a strand of hair stuck in my lip gloss. A few yards away, someone honked on a trumpet. A group of girls cheered. Sounds of celebration. Then Beau smiled. He actually smiled at me.

"I just wanted to say congratulations. You totally deserve to be valedictorian."

An air horn wailed, and I flinched. The tang of copper flooded my mouth. It tasted like suspicion. Was this guy joking? Beau's half a foot taller than me, so I tweaked my neck just looking up at him. His chestnut-colored hair was messy from his graduation cap. Waves of it swooped into his eyes. They were the color of the lake. Like mossy water. I saw no trace of teasing in them.

Hmm.

He stuck out his hand. "No hard feelings?"

I was half expecting Beau might be hiding some kind of buzzer in his palm to zap me, but I let him take my hand anyway. And oh, wow! Did I ever get zapped. But not from any hidden buzzer. Just from Beau's touch. His whole hand wrapped around mine, so warm and strong, I felt like my fingers might fall off. I yanked back and looked down at the ground.

"Thanks, Beau," I mumbled.

"Listen. I've been kind of a jerk these past few years. And I'm really sorry. If you'll accept my apology, I have something I want to give you. Call it a peace offering before we both leave for college."

I lifted my chin to meet his gaze, and my stomach swooped. *Hey, guy. Don't look at me all warm and sincere. Aren't you aware I hate you?* But he was being so nice. Maybe I shouldn't look a gift horse in the mouth. Or in those big, lakey eyes. "I mean, I guess that's fine," I stammered.

"I don't want Brady to see us though." He shifted his weight. "You know how it is with him."

I tilted my head. "No. How is it?"

Beau's brows pulled together. "Your brother doesn't exactly want me hanging with you." He glanced around. Was he actually nervous? "Maybe you could meet me back behind the gym."

"Just the two of us?" When I started blushing, Beau's mouth tipped up on one side.

"Don't worry." He chuckled. "I'm not going to try to kiss you, Kasey. Please. You're like my sister."

Sister. Gross.

Beau's actual sister, Natalie, was a year younger than me, and even meaner than Beau. Ugh. Still. His insult did give me an idea. So I told Beau I'd meet him behind the gym. Then I shrugged like I didn't much care. I told myself I didn't much care.

But maybe Brady would.

If my brother found out Beau Slater was giving me some kind

of graduation gift, it might really freak him out. That could be good right? One last way for me to get my brother's goat before I left for college. And what if I *could* get Beau to kiss me? Brady might absolutely implode. Of course, *I* didn't want to kiss Beau Slater.

But I sure did want revenge on Brady Graham.

When my mom tried to wrangle the whole family for pictures, I told her I had to run to the bathroom first. Then I sneaked away to slip off my graduation gown before my meet up with Beau. Underneath the gown, I wore a brand new dress, and not to brag, but the dress looked good. The material was silky soft and sky blue. The color really brought out my eyes. And if I was going to tempt Beau Slater, having eyes like the sky was a good first step.

More cherry lip gloss was the second. Three layers thick. Pucker. Blot. *Ready.*

With a tickle of butterflies in my stomach, I sneaked behind the gym all by myself. The red brick building was quiet in the shadow of late afternoon. Beau was just a few yards away, waiting for me under a cluster of dense pines. The grass below him had given way to dirt. A single ray of sunlight played across his face. He looked up and saw me.

"Hey," he said.

"Hey, yourself." As he approached, I licked my lips hoping to make them shiny enough to kiss. And as it turns out, cherry lip gloss doesn't taste nearly as delicious as it looks. I must've made a face, because Beau reached out for me.

"Are you okay?"

I nodded as he closed the space between us. Then he guided me back below the trees. A bird burst from the branches, cawing as it hit the sky. My tongue was knotted up tight, like the rope tying Uncle Cubby's boat to the dock. At this point, Beau was so near to me, I was practically swimming in his scent. Citrus and spice. Salty and sweet. I wanted to bury my face in his neck.

Where did that feeling come from? No, no, no. This was not part of the plan. I was here to collect Beau's gift, get my kiss, then tell Brady about both. He'd freak out and be furious with Beau. Two birds killed with one lip lock.

I bent my face up and closed my eyes, moving toward him inch by inch. My heart was a hammer in my chest. How would Beau's lips feel? Would they be warm? Soft? Would he take me in his arms? I felt a hand at my waist. He was touching me. Beau Slater was touching me! My eyes flew open, and I saw our noses were practically touching. I could taste the peppermint on his breath. And in that moment, I realized this wasn't about Brady.

I wanted this kiss. I did.

That's when I heard laughter ringing from above. Beau jumped back, and a split second later, the first water balloon struck. Then another. And another. I was being pelted in big wet slaps. Splash. Splash! SPLASH! I stood there, gaping and frozen, while my special-occasion hair got soaked. Water streamed down my face into my mouth. Lip gloss and mascara streaked my chin. I looked up, and there was Brady, crouched in the tree, clutching a bucket.

He and Beau had set me up.

Humiliated and horrified, I unstuck my feet and began to run. I kept on running all the way to the docks. Then I hid on my uncle's boat the rest of the night. I couldn't face my brother or his smug satisfaction. Thanks to Brady and Beau, I missed graduation pictures. I missed our family dinner. When I finally dragged myself home, my parents were beyond hurt and furious. I'd scared them so much, but I was too embarrassed to explain. I couldn't tell my parents what a fool I'd been, so I got in trouble. Big trouble. My usually-patient father grounded me, and I didn't even argue. I broke my mother's heart that night.

But mine was already broken.

Five years later, I stand in my bedroom, and my stomach does backflips remembering. Not much has changed since those days of solitary confinement. Not my comforter or my Nick Cage pillow. Pictures from Homecoming and Prom are taped along my mirror. I'd gone to both dances with my best friends. Molly,

Claire, and Emma. Two corsages still sit in a jewelry dish. They're both dried up and dusty now. When I pick the carnation up to sniff it, the petals crumble.

Sliding open my nightstand drawer, I pull out a pristine copy of *Twilight*. The rest of my family hated all things *Twilight*, so I knew they'd never open that book. Tucked inside the pages is a picture of Beau Slater. A candid of him in his baseball uniform after our team won the league championship. That's right. A girl doesn't get to be in charge of the school yearbook without gaining access to photographs that never see the light of day. Beau was the pitcher for the Abieville Lancers. Brady played first base. Beau's grinning at someone off camera. Probably my stupid brother. Beau looks so happy in the picture. Too bad someone drew devil horns and buck teeth on his face. In Sharpie.

KGS.

Kasey Graham's Sharpie.

"Kasey! Are you home?" Auntie Mae out calls to me. She must've been the one banging around in the kitchen. Not Brady and Beau preparing to water-balloon me again. I slip the picture of Beau back into *Twilight*, then shove the book back into the nightstand. My permanent hatred is safe and sound again. A secret between Bella, Edward, and me.

As I enter the kitchen, the scent of cinnamon almost bowls me over. Every Christmas, my mom keeps sticks of it simmering on the stove. Of course she'd do it even in July. Auntie Mae's bent over the bottom shelf of the fridge now, her rear end straining the seams of her shorts. There's an American flag emblazoned across the seat, which must be some kind of crime against fashion, if not the nation.

As she straightens and turns, she shrieks. "Ack!" Her cheeks turn red like the puff of hair on her head. All the Bradford sisters, and most of their kids, have hair that's some shade of red, but Auntie Mae wins the gold medal of poodle cuts. "You surprised me," she gasps. "I almost dropped the rack of ribs on the linoleum."

My shoulders creep up. "Sorry, Auntie Mae."

"Well. No harm, no foul." With a huff and a grunt, she sets the ribs in a pan on the counter. Then she turns back to me. "You're a sight for sore eyes, Kasey. We've sure been missing you around here."

"I miss everyone, too, Auntie Mae. So much."

"Let me rinse off my hands so we can hug. I don't want to get beef juice all over you."

"Yeah." I grin. "I don't want that either."

She runs her hands under the faucet then dries them on Mom's Frosty the Snowman dishtowel. "Now get on over here." She opens her arms wide and pulls me into her not-unsubstantial bosom. Auntie Mae smells more like nutmeg than beef juice, and I try to let myself relax. Maybe if I stay busy making potato salad and snickerdoodles, I'll be able to stop thinking about Beau.

After an epic hug, my aunt gets to work prepping the ribs, and I get to work peeling potatoes. Our sink is a big porcelain basin on a butcher block island in the center of the kitchen. This means from where I'm standing, I can see the entire room. I'm elbow deep in peel when my mother comes barreling around the corner. "Ah! There you are, Kasey."

"Here I am. Right where you told me to be. Peeling potatoes."

My mother turns to Auntie Mae. "How are the ribs coming along?"

"I basted them up, and they're in the oven now. I was about to head to The Shop to get the corn. I wanted the ears to be as fresh as possible."

"Thanks, Mae," my mom says, and the two of them exchange glances.

"Don't worry," Auntie Mae says. "I'll get all the cobs they have." It's like they've got an unspoken language between them. I always wished I had a sister who knew what I was trying to say without words.

"I'll only be gone about a half hour," my aunt says.

"Don't worry," I snort. "I'll still be here peeling potatoes. I might be peeling for the rest of my life."

As soon as Auntie Mae's out the back door, Mom joins me at the sink. She fills an enormous pot with water and sets it on the counter beside her. "Sorry for dropping that bomb earlier about Beau Slater being in town. I thought you knew."

"Why would I know?" My heart pounds, but I just keep peeling at a furious pace. "I couldn't care less, I was just surprised. I thought Beau was some globetrotting hero with a camera, off saving humanity or something." I shrug. "Like Superman or Gandhi."

My mother sucks in a breath. "Superman's not real, Kasey. And as for Gandhi ..." She lowers her voice. "He's passed."

"I was kidding, Mom. You get jokes, right?"

She huffs out a breath. "My daughter. The standup comedian."

That's right. I'm still not a doctor, Mother.

She starts picking up the peeled potatoes and cutting them up into quarters. Once they're cut, she drops them in the pot. "Anyway, you're partly right," she says. "According to Betty Slater, Beau's been taking pictures all around the world. She says he donates a lot of the proceeds to charities. One is for food banks, I think. And clean drinking water. That kind of thing. I suppose he *is* pretty heroic, now that you mention it."

"Did I mention he was heroic?" I sniff. "Hmm. Whatever. Good for Beau."

"Good for Betty," my mom says. "She's just thrilled to have both her kids under one roof at the same time."

"Oh!" The peeler flies out of my hand and clatters into the sink. "Natalie's here too?"

"Of course, dear. She's home for the whole summer."

Natalie Slater, Beau's little sister, always had it out for me. I never knew why she hated me so much, but she once threatened to serve me brownies baked with Ex-Lax. Needless to say, I steered clear of her after that. Mom plucks the peeler from the sink and gives it back to me, along with a healthy dose of side-eye. "Are you all right, Kasey?"

"I'm fantastic," I chirp. "So, you were saying, Nat's home for the summer. What's she been up to?"

"Betty says she'll be finishing her undergrad this year, and then she's getting a degree in nursing." My mother examines a potato with a smudge of dirt on it. She takes her time rinsing the potato before she resumes her slicing. "Apparently she's planning to work in pediatrics. In cancer wards, I think."

"Wow. Another Slater hero." I glance at my mother.

"Betty's a little worried Natalie will want to move out west. Like you."

"Oh, wow." I wrinkle my nose. "I hope she doesn't."

"Why ever would you say that?"

"When we were kids, Beau and Nat Slater were pretty awful to me, Mom."

She raises an eyebrow. "I didn't think Beau was all that bad."

"Oh, come on, Mom." I resume peeling to avoid her gaze. "He and Brady were terrible."

She shakes her head. Cluck. *Mrs. Chicken Claus is back.* "Maybe when you were kids. But your brother's grown up quite a bit in the past few years. He's become a good man. And Betty says Beau has really come into his own too. You'll see."

"I can't wait," I mumble.

My mother hefts the pot up and carries it to the stove. "You know Beau's like you."

"What?" Gah! I almost slice off my finger with the peeler. "Beau *likes* me?"

"I said, he's *like* you. Barely home." There's a whoosh from the stovetop as the gas burner ignites. "And by next week, he'll be gone again. Poof." I look over my shoulder, and my mother shakes her head. "Poor Betty."

"Sounds like you and Mrs. Slater have been talking quite a bit lately. When did you two become so friendly?"

"Oh, I don't know." She sighs. "Maybe after we both had one of our birdies leave the nest and hardly ever come back."

Huh. I guess my mother misses me even though I'm not a doctor. Or a standup comedian for that matter. "Mom." I wait for her to meet my gaze. "I really *am* happy to be home."

She smiles. "I'm happy about that too. And before I forget, Betty and I made plans for all eight of us to watch the fireworks over at their place on the 4th. So be sure you're free."

My stomach twists, but my mom can't see that. "What if I wanted to see Molly? Or Emma? Or Claire?" I'm blurting out names in a strangled rasp.

"You can see them at the A-Fair, Kasey. The rest of this week is about family." My mother resumes cutting potatoes like she didn't just blow up my life. "Betty and Neil still live in the house right on the lake. I imagine the fireworks are quite a spectacle from their yard. Did you ever watch over there, Kasey?"

"Are you kidding?" I swallow hard. "Brady never let me be around him and Beau." A flush comes into my cheeks. "Not that I ever wanted to be around him and Beau." Stupid cheeks. They always give me away. Unless my throat gets there first.

"Well, you're going to be around them plenty this week." *Tsk.* "I already told Betty we'd all go, and the Grahams always follow through on their RSVPs. Also, I invited the Slaters here tomorrow night for hot cocoa and caroling with your cousins."

WHAAAAAAT?

Now my insides officially explode. Why are the Grahams and the Slaters suddenly attached at the hip? I want my hips as far from Beau's as they can get. I flash my mother a desperate look, but she's got her eyes glued to her knife. "Are you really going to let Beau Slater ruin my 4th of July *and* Christmas?" I choke out.

"Don't be dramatic, Kasey." Her lip curls up on one side, and it sounds like she's actually humming. What on earth is happening? My mother's on my side.

Isn't she?

BEAU

"Thanks for the help," Brady says. "And for the ride. Don't quote me, but I missed you, man."

I flash him a crooked smile. "Too late. Already sent out a press release."

"Ahh. So I'll have to murder you now, then. Got no choice."

Brady and I are in my dad's truck on the way back from the docks. We met up this morning at his parents' place so I could say hi. They were out front when I got there, Mr. Graham chopping wood and Mrs. Graham stacking. Brady was grumbling about having to clean the kayaks, so I offered to help him out. By way of answer, he just hopped in the truck.

Typical Brady.

"Honestly, being back at the lake felt good." I lick my lips and taste the salt of my sweat. The place was still crowded when we left, full of boats pulling inner tubes and water skiers. It felt like I'd jumped off that dock only yesterday. And forever ago. Give or take.

"When we get back, you want to come in for a drink?" Brady offers. "My old man's got coolers stocked for a week. Besides. I owe you one."

"Nah. I was happy to do it." Turning onto the tree-lined road that winds around the back side of town, I check my watch. Four o'clock. "It's a little early for me anyway."

"I was talking about soda." Brady punches my arm. "But when did you become such a grownup?"

I crack another smile. "One of us has to be an adult. I nominated you, but ..."

He smirks. "It didn't go too well?"

"I didn't say that. But how did a goof-off kid like you manage to land a real-life job with Doc Swanson? Working at a vet clinic is serious business."

Brady chuckles. "I rely on my charms, man."

I arch an eyebrow. "You?"

"Hey. I can be charming when I want to be. You just forgot because you've been gone so long."

"Sure, sure. I remember. You're definitely charming. A real prince."

He snorts. "According to my mom, you're the *real* prince of the village. You should hear how she raves about you." Brady switches to a high-pitched warble that's a decent imitation of Mrs. Graham. "Beau is so amazing, Brady. His little photography hobby is *so* impressive."

"Little photography hobby?" I give Brady the side eye, but I get why he'd bust my chops. He has no idea what my career means to me. How proud I am of what we do. I don't share those feelings with anybody. The only one I ever wanted to share things with is way out of reach.

"And don't forget all the charities Beau supports," Brady screeches. He's still using his mother's voice. "My word, Brady! Think of the children!" He keeps going like that until we reach the Grahams' house. Luckily it's not a long drive.

When I pull up for the second time today, I flash back to the gut twists I'd get here back in high school. Half dread, half expectation. Then I remind myself Kasey doesn't live in Abieville anymore. She doesn't even live in the state.

"At least come in for a minute," Brady says. "My mom's probably baking snickerdoodles by now." He takes a beat. "In honor of your illustrious return."

"All right." I duck my head like I'm eighteen again. "I've got some time, I guess."

And Mrs. Graham's cookies really are the best.

We climb the steps up to their porch and kick our flip flops off next to the welcome mat. *Kiss Me Under the Mistletoe.* Huh. What's up with that? And why is there a wreath on the door?

We head inside, and I catch the scent of an eggnog candle. There's a massive tree by the fireplace. "Uh, Brady?" I survey the room. It looks like Santa Claus threw up everywhere. "Should I be worried?"

"Crazy, right?" He flops on the couch and props his feet on the coffee table. "All I can say is I'm glad I moved out." He smirks. "Just in the St. Nick of time."

"No, but seriously. We were together all day, and you failed to mention your parents turned their house into the North Pole. What gives?"

He chuckles. "It's my mom's brilliant idea. She talked all my out-of-town cousins into coming home for the 4th of July. And since a lot of them weren't around for Christmas—and my mother's a total nut job—she's got the whole family decking the halls. A double-duty holiday."

"Right." I rake a hand through my hair. It's still damp from the lake. "No one says no to Elaine Graham."

"Heh. You remember." He clears his throat, and looks down at his hands. "Anyway, it's not just about my mom being ridiculous. We're also kind of hoping the traditions will be nice for my grandma and my aunt, you know?"

"Yeah." I shift my weight. "I'm really sorry about your grandpa. And your uncle."

"Thanks, man." His voice is thick and low. Emotional. Very un-Brady. "Me too." He cuts his gaze to the coffee table. There's a hairband in the center, and he scrambles to sit up. "Ahhh!" His eyes are bright now. "Kasey must be home."

Kasey. My stomach clenches like a fist. A total gut punch. Multiple punches. "Your sister's in town?"

Before he can answer, Mrs. Graham careens out of the kitchen. "I thought I heard men talking in here." She makes eye contact with me. "And I'm gonna need another hug." She swings toward me like a wrecking ball, and the next thing I know, I'm being crushed by Brady's mom. She's changed out of her wood-stacking gear into full Christmas mode. Her hair's in a big red pile on top of her head. I almost can't see past her while she's squeezing me.

"Kasey!" she hollers toward the kitchen. "Get in here and say hi to Beau!"

Kasey comes around the corner slowly, and *Whoa*. My lungs empty out in one quick whoosh. Her hair's a little longer than I remember. Not that I thought about her every day for the past five years. Except I did. That's why I know her eyes are the same. So bright they could be the sun. Twin stars that never saw how I felt about her. I never let anyone see.

While I'm gasping for air, she waves at me. It's a small one. So is her frown. "Hey there, Beau."

I open my mouth, but I can't speak. The good news is I don't have to, because Brady's off the couch and over to Kasey in a flash. He picks up his sister and spins her around like she's light as a feather. They're practically flying. When he sets her down, Kasey stumbles my way. She's Bambi on ice. I catch her in my arms.

"Oof," I say as Kasey crashes into me. At least I'm making noise with my mouth again. It's not a good noise, but it's better than nothing. When I pull her in, I smell cherries and sunshine. Like we're on a beach. In Santa's village.

"You all right?" I ask. My question comes out gruff like I'm choking on sand.

"I'm fine." She wrenches herself from me and rounds on Brady. "Were you *trying* to make me fall?"

Brady grins. "Can't a guy be excited to see his little sister?"

She cocks her head. "Not when the guy is you."

"Really, Kase." His voice is thick with emotion again. Who *is* this guy and what did he do with Brady? "I missed you," he says. "A lot."

Kasey's eyes soften, but she works her jaw like she definitely can't trust us. Which makes sense. The last time all three of us were together, Brady was attacking her with water balloons. She was shivering. Wet. Crying. My insides crank like a vise at the memory.

"Oh, my babies." Mrs. Graham grabs Kasey with one arm, then yanks Brady in with the other. I stand there, feeling like an idiot, while the three of them are mashed together. "Having you both home makes me so happy," she says. "I wish I could hug you like this for the whole week. I suppose I can. Oh, but Brady." She pulls away. "You'll need to run back to your place and change soon."

Brady looks down at his swim trunks and bare feet. "I think I'm good. Suit's almost dry."

Mrs. Graham puts her hands on her hips. "Did you remember to bring your ugly sweater?"

Now *that* gets me talking again. "What's this about an ugly sweater, Brady?"

Mrs. Graham answers for him. "Tonight's our Ugly Sweater Dinner, Beau. It's a competition. The ugliest sweater wins. Did you ever come to one when you and Brady were kids?"

I dart a glance at Kasey. "Can't say that I did."

"Well, that's just one of the things I've got planned for Christmas in July." She digs in her apron pocket and retrieves a wrinkled paper. "I sketched out a schedule for the week. It's a little rough, still." She shoves her reading glasses up her nose. "Let's see. Ugly Sweater Dinner and tree trimming is tonight. Tomorrow is cocoa and caroling." She glances up at me. "By the way, Beau. You, Natalie, and your folks are coming over for that."

I gulp like the Polar Express just rolled into the living room to pick me up. "We are?"

"Your mom and I planned it. We're going to have so much

fun!" Mrs. Graham checks her schedule again. "The next day, everyone will be here decorating gingerbread houses. I was thinking we could make that a competition, too, but the 4th of July parade floats are being judged that day." She peers at me over her glasses. "What do you think, Beau? Is that too much competition?"

"I think—"

"You're right." She wrinkles her nose. "I think it's too much. Anyway, the next day is the parade and the picnic for the 4th. Then we'll be coming to your folks' place afterward to watch the fireworks together."

Another train pulls up to the station. All aboard. "You will?"

"Yes." She waves her list like she's waking me up. "After the parade, Beau. Try to keep up."

Brady smirks. "You and Mrs. Slater sure have been busy making plans, huh, Mom?"

By now, my head's officially spinning. This is a lot of information to take in after finding out Kasey Graham is in the same town as me. Scratch that. She's in the same *room* with me. And it sounds like we're going to be together a whole lot more this week.

How did that happen? Who's in charge here?

Mrs. Graham bobs her head. "You're absolutely right, Beau."

Wait. Did I say something out loud? Something that was absolutely right?

"We've got too many activities to keep track of." Mrs. Graham glances at Brady. "Especially for those who struggle with time management. But I've got an idea." She snaps her fingers. A real light bulb moment. "Kasey can make a big poster of this schedule to hang on the wall for everyone's reference. You'll do that for me, won't you, Kasey?" Mrs. Graham doesn't wait for a response. She just shoves the paper at her.

Kasey's eyes go extra wide. She looks pretty blindsided. I know the feeling. "Sure, Mom." She shifts her weight from one foot to the other. Doc Martens. Nice. Cut off shorts and tan legs. Nicer.

Mrs. Graham claps her hands together just once. But loudly. "Well, then, I suppose I'll just go finish up the potato salad."

"Hey, Mom." Brady raises his hand like we're back in sixth grade and she's our teacher. "Are the snickerdoodles ready yet?"

"No. So before you get your ugly sweater, I need you to come to the kitchen to open up some mayonnaise for me. I figure three jars ought to do it."

Brady snorts. "That's a lot of mayo for cookies, Mom."

She frowns. "It's for the potato salad. Now, come on. Let me borrow your muscles."

"Still sounds like too much mayo," he says.

"Brady, now!" Without waiting for a response, she charges back into the kitchen.

Brady looks at me and shrugs. "Sorry, man. Guess I'll catch you later." Then he leaves me alone with his sister.

Kasey Elizabeth Graham.

Oh, man. I've told myself a million times I'd be over her the next time I saw her. But here we are. And I'm so not over her. I am way, way under. For a couple of beats, we both stand there, saying nothing. When the heat starts creeping up my neck, I wish I had an ugly Christmas sweater on to hide it.

"So, Beau." Kasey breaks the silence, but there's an edge to her voice. A sharpness. "I hear you're back from saving humanity," she says. "One picture at a time."

I duck my head. "Something like that." I was aiming for humble, but I probably sound like a jerk. I'm epically blowing it, and I don't know how to make it better. Then again, I can't make things much worse.

She raises an eyebrow. "So where in the world are you off to next? What's on the big hero's agenda?"

I clear my throat. "I'm in between gigs at the moment." This is technically true, although I've been coordinating my next freelance assignment for months. It's a real score, partnering with a Pulitzer Prize winning photographer. A once in a lifetime opportunity. But right now, I just want to hang out in this living room with Kasey. "Anyway, I've got some free time on my hands." I nod at the wrinkled paper. "I could probably help out with that poster."

Kasey cocks her head. "With what?"

"The holiday schedule your mom asked you to make. I can help. But only if you—"

"Fine." She chews her bottom lip. Then she disappears down the hall. Cabinets squeak open and slam shut. When she returns, she's got a roll of butcher paper, a box of colored markers, tape, and scissors. "Here you go." She sets the supplies on the coffee table. "I'll be back in a half hour to check your work. This is important to my mom, so try not to screw it up."

She spins on a heel, and I watch her head up the stairs.

Wait. What just happened here, Beau?

Wow. She still really hates me. And I'm stuck here, fighting some battle between wanting to fix things with her and needing to stay loyal to Brady. He'd kill me if he knew half the stuff I've thought about his sister over the years. Now I just have to get through this week. Then I'll be gone again. And Kasey can go back to being a memory.

In the meantime, I said I'd help her out. So I hike up my board shorts and drop to my knees in front of the butcher paper. How different can making a poster be from making photographs? It's all art, right? I take a beat. Wait for inspiration. Something to give me an idea of how to begin ... *Nope. Nada. Nothing.*

That's all right. Like any new task, I won't get anywhere without diving in, so I open the markers and the top of the box rips off in my hand. Great.

Strike one, Beau.

Moving on. This is a holiday schedule, so I should probably use the red and green markers for Christmas and the red and blue ones for the 4th of July. But markers feel too permanent. Glancing around the room, I look for a pencil to trace with. *Nope. Nada. Nothing.*

Perfect. Markers it is. I pick the blue one first—like Kasey's

33

eyes—and draw a straight line across the top of the paper. When I'm done, though, my straight line looks more like a ski slope.

Strike two, Beau.

I shove the blue marker back in the box, thinking I'll have better luck with red. I pop off the cap, and it smells like cherries, which reminds me of Kasey's lips right before we almost kissed. And just like that, she reappears, coming down the stairs.

It's like she can hear inside my head. Like she's magic. Maybe she *is*. She sure looks magical right now. Her shorts and boots are gone, and she's changed into a sundress. Green like an emerald. Like my favorite part of *The Wizard of Oz*. Her hair's hanging over her shoulder in a loose braid. A braid of fire.

I drop the marker.

"How's it going, Beau?" I open my mouth to answer her, but my throat's gone bone dry. "That bad, huh?" Kasey frowns. "Here. Let me take a look." She hovers over me, and I look up at her, but instead of checking out my total failure of a poster, she searches my eyes for a full five seconds. Then she starts cracking up. In my face.

"Oh my gosh, Beau! You should see yourself right now." She stifles a laugh and ends up snorting. "Did you actually think I was going to leave you in charge of my mom's poster thing?"

"Uhhh ... I ..."

"Oh. My. Whoa." She shakes her head.

"Yep." I bob my head. "I'm an idiot."

"Saving humanity must've fried your brain."

Sure. That's what did it. This has nothing to do with you.

Kasey bends over to pick up the marker I dropped at the exact same time Brady strolls in from the kitchen.

"Hey." He cocks his head. "What's going on here?" I leap to my feet so fast I almost knock Kasey over. But I grab her wrist just in time. As she regains her footing, Brady comes toward us, eyes darting back and forth. "Were you just ... hitting on my sister?"

"No way, man." I put a hand up. "I was just—"

"Dude." He breaks into a grin. "I'm kidding."

"Okay. Sure. Cool. Cool." My whole face burns, and Brady turns to Kasey.

"Check this guy out, Kase." He cackles. "My boy Beau here is squirming like I was about to punch his lights out."

She shrugs like she wouldn't care if her brother decked me. *Great.* I force a smile even though three quarters of the Graham family are straight-up killing me. Any minute now, Mr. Graham's going to show up and accuse me of drinking all the soda in his cooler. So I make a show of checking my watch.

"Oh, hey. Look at the time. I promised Natalie I'd get the truck back before dinner. We're sharing it this week, and she needs it to go out."

"What's she up to?" Brady asks.

Uh. Deer in headlights. "Something that requires a truck. Which we're sharing. As I said. But if I'm any later ... well ..."

"What would Nat do?" Kasey tilts her head. "Put Ex-Lax in your brownies?"

"Ha! Brownies! Right!" I try on a laugh, even though I have no idea what Kasey's talking about. "Anyway, I need to get going." But the truth is I don't need to get going. I need to get a grip. Then I need to get it through my thick skull that having feelings for Kasey Graham is impossible.

First of all, she's obviously still mad at me. And Brady obviously doesn't want me anywhere near his sister. Still. Add those together, and Kasey's off-limits. Way off.

Always has been. Always will be.

I'm about to show everyone how way-off-limits Kasey Graham is by taking off and never coming back, when Mr. Graham barges through the front door. He's sporting nutty professor hair, a pair of cargo shorts, and a golf shirt. Under his Birkenstocks he's got on a pair of socks that reach his knees. He's also weighed down by at least a dozen cartons of butter.

"Daddy!" Kasey rushes over to hug her father and his butter.

"Hey there, sweetheart," he says. "It's about time you got here. Did you know you're late for Christmas?"

"Good to see you too, Dad." She kisses his cheek, and I almost feel jealous. Of Phillip Graham. And his cheek. I am definitely off my game.

"Beau!" he bellows. "Great to see you again. Twice in one day, huh?"

"Yep." *Lucky me.* "Can I help you with that butter, sir?"

"Oh, no, no." He chuckles. "I think I've got everything pretty well-balanced." He glances at Kasey and Brady. "Don't you make any sudden moves either, or this Tower of Pisa here might topple."

I take a step toward the door, preparing to make my escape. "In that case, I'll be heading out."

"Hold on, son." Mr. Graham jams his chin on the leaning tower of butter so it won't fall. "Leaving so soon?"

"I regret that truck-sharing-duty calls." *I regret that truck-sharing-duty calls?* Why am I talking like this? When did I become Nathan Hale? "Anyway, have a good one." To add to my weirdness, I salute the Grahams because apparently I can't stop being an idiot.

"All righty then, Beau," Mr. Graham says. "My better half tells me we'll be seeing your family for the cocoa and caroling shindig tomorrow."

I blow out a breath. "Wouldn't miss it, sir."

Kasey pipes up. "You'd better start preparing your song, Beau."

"Preparing my what?"

"Oh. Didn't my mom tell you?" Her mouth tilts up on one side. "Everyone has to take at least one turn leading a carol."

"Sure, sure. Cool." I run a hand through my hair. "I get it. This is another one of your jokes, right?"

Brady smirks. "Nope. That's the rule, man. And I already got dibs on 'O Holy Night.' I like to really nail those high notes, so don't even think about picking that one."

"Don't worry. I wouldn't dream of it."

But I might have a nightmare tonight.

Chapter Four

A TEXT THREAD WITH THE MCCOYS BEFORE THE UGLY SWEATER DINNER

Kasey: Hey, cousins! SO sorry I missed you all last night, but I can't wait to see everyone soon. Any chance someone over there has an extra ugly sweater I can borrow?
Olivia: I only packed one (under duress) and wearing this thing seriously hurts my soul not to mention my eyes. Like literally. I can't look in a mirror right now, or I'll have a total identity crisis. Who started this tradition, and when can we let it die?
Darby: It's OK, Liv. No one here cares what you look like, and my five Instagram followers are too busy worrying about getting into med school someday to share my post in their stories. Probably. PS: That's not how the word LITERALLY works.
Olivia: YOU POSTED A PIC ON INSTAGRAM?
Darby: Please tell me the Denver altitude hasn't killed every last one of your brain cells.
Tess: Liv. Darby is LITERALLY joking. <skull emoji>
Olivia: You're hilarious, Darbs. Consider this a retraction of any and all invitations to visit me before school starts. That honor is reserved for my favorite sister now.
Darby: You only like Tess more than me because she dresses worse than you.
Tess: HEY!

Olivia: Everyone dresses worse than I do. And I was only kidding, too, Darbs. You aren't the only family member with a sense of humor. You and your inferior wardrobe can still come to the beauteous mountains of Colorado with Tess and me. Just don't wear your ugly sweater. Please.
Darby: I was joking about Instagram, but not about med school. I've got an internship lined up that I need for my applications. I can't take a vacation after this one. <crying emoji>
Tess: On that note, I've been meaning to tell you, I don't think I can make it this summer either, Liv.
Olivia: WHYYYYY? (Yes. That was a whine-font.)
Tess: I'm studying for the LSATs. Plus, now that Mom moved, I have to help Mac out with Daisy.
Mac: You don't have to help me out with Daisy. Or in with Daisy. And I'm going to win tonight, so don't even bother borrowing an ugly sweater, Kase.
Darby: Why is Mac on this thread?
Kasey: I added him.
Mac: I'm a McCoy cousin too. I was the first one, actually.
Olivia: Exactly. Aren't you a little old to be participating in an ugly sweater contest? Once you have a kid of your own, I feel like stepping down should be mandatory.
Mac: Afraid to lose?
Olivia: An ugly sweater contest? HA. I'm afraid to win.
Mac: You won't. Look at me.
Olivia: You are pretty hideous.
Kasey: Hold on. Are the four of you together in the same room right now? Why are you all texting instead of talking?
Darby: You started the thread, Kasey.
Kasey: True. But I didn't expect you to start discussing all your future sibling plans on it. (LOL!)
Olivia: Apparently there ARE no future sibling plans, because nobody loves me. My sisters are clearly too threatened by my beauty.
Mac: You're triplets. You three are all equally unattractive to me.

Olivia: Sick burn, Mac.
Darby: Nah. It's cool that Liv is the pretty one. I got all the brains.
Tess: What did I get all of?
Mac: Me.
Tess: Pass.
Mac: Daisy?
Tess: I was thinking more along the lines of a scintillating personality. You people couldn't last a minute without my particular brand of sunshine.
Darby: False.
Olivia: What you've got is a closet full of ugly sweaters, Tess. You *must* have an extra one for Kasey.
Tess: I don't have ugly sweaters. I just have sweaters.
Olivia: *cough* ugly *cough.
Tess: Fine. I'll bring one over now, Kase. I gotta get out of this house anyway.
Kasey: Thanks, Tess. PS: My mom wants me to remind you all to be here at 6:00 sharp (LOL)!

I hit send and set down my phone with a huge smile on my face. Even better, the smile sticks around while I finish up the poster for my mom. But the *best* part about my good mood is that I barely think about Beau Slater. No more than once or twice. And even then, I'm still grinning. But that's only because I'm excited to see my cousins. Not because of Beau.
At all.

Chapter Five

ELAINE GRAHAM'S CHRISTMAS IN JULY HOLIDAY SCHEDULE!

July 1st: Ugly Sweater Dinner and Tree Trimming!
July 2nd: Cocoa and Christmas Caroling!
July 3rd: Gingerbread House Decorating!
July 4th: Picnic, Parade, and Fireworks!
July 5th: Christmas Eve Breakfast, Lunch, and Pajamas!
July 6th: Christmas Day and the A-Fair ... If You Dare!
Saturday, July 7th: Kasey Returns to LA and Her Brand New Job!

*Poster Made by Kasey, but Don't Blame Her!
(Especially for all the exclamation points ...)*

Chapter Six

KASEY

In case you were waiting on the edge of your seat for the results of our Ugly Sweater Competition, I didn't win. My cousin Mac and his snowman monstrosity took home that sweet, sweet prize. That is, if one of Auntie Ann's fruitcakes can be considered any kind of trophy.

But after dinner, when we trimmed the tree, I won the unofficial award for the most broken ornaments. I had a grand total of three, but only one of the casualties was my fault. The others came out of the box cracked.

Auntie Ann blamed Uncle Irv for those first two, claiming he roughed up the box with his "big ham hands." To prove I had no hard feelings, I topped off my uncle's eggnog, but then I accidentally dropped my teddy bear ornament. Its head snapped off on the hardwoods.

Three broken ornaments: Check!

The teddy beheading might've made me sadder if I hadn't been sure the bear ornament was actually Brady's. When he handed it to me last night, he was being unusually nice, so I didn't want to argue with him. But I distinctly remember wishing I'd gotten a teddy bear that year instead of the ornament I did get—

which was a hippopotamus. Who even makes a Christmas ornament out of a hippo? I'm just saying. It's not a bad question.

Ornament catastrophes aside, the rest of the night went off without a hitch, except that my cousin Ford couldn't join us. He's a firefighter who's on-call on weekends. But since he lives here in Abieville full time, his absence wasn't a deal breaker. Everyone agreed the bigger coup was finally getting all four of Aunt Remy's kids—and her one, non-talking grandchild—here at the same time.

Mac is not only the oldest of the cousins, he's also the only one with a kid. Not to mention the only one who's ever been married, and then divorced. But everyone usually acts like his ex never existed. Don't feel too bad for Gwen, though. She abandoned Mac and Daisy last year on Daisy's birthday. There's probably no such thing as a *good* time to leave your family, but on your four-year-old daughter's birthday?

That's next-level worst.

They're still getting over that heartbreak, but we're all hoping Mac will meet someone wonderful soon. Someone who'll give him and Daisy the love they deserve. That's a lot, for the record.

Besides Mac, Aunt Remy also has the triplets: Darby, Olivia, and Tess. The girls are the last of the ten cousins. That's because once the other three Bradford sisters realized they might end up with surprise multiples, they stopped making children. Triplets aren't necessarily problematic in and of themselves. And the McCoy girls are seriously awesome. But a lot of the houses in Abieville are turn-of-the-century, and still only have one full bathroom. So having fewer kids just makes good sense.

Something that *doesn't* make sense—but definitely reveals everything you need to know about my mother and her sisters—is that all four of them have sons named Bradford. Can you just imagine how those phone calls from the delivery room went?

Aunt Remy: Ted and I named our boy Bradford!
Auntie Mae: Cubby and I named our boy Bradford!
Auntie Ann: Irv and I named our boy Bradford!

My mom: Guess what Phil and I named the baby!

To keep the four Bradford boys straight, they all have different nicknames. Mac is Mac because of his last name. Next up is Three, whose nickname would be more logical if Three had been the third boy named Bradford. But he was the second. Nobody seems to notice or care. Ford is the actual third Bradford boy. Then came Brady. He's the last one. And it comes as no surprise to me that my brother broke that particular mold.

Of course there's a whole other mold for the girls. Six of us in total. You already know about the triplets. Then there's Three's sister, Nella. Originally Penelope. She belongs to Auntie Mae and Uncle Cubby. Ford's sister is Felicity. We call her Letty. She belongs to Auntie Ann and Uncle Irv.

Would a flow chart be handy?

Just kidding. I don't have a flow chart. I used up all my poster-making skills yesterday. What I *do* have is *The Official List of Carols* our group will be singing tonight. That's right. I'm standing in the doorway with a clipboard to add songs to the list as everyone arrives. The carolers who are already here are inside sipping hot cocoa even though it's eighty-five degrees out.

I wipe a bead of sweat from my brow. Why did my mother put me in charge of the music? I can't even carry a tune to save my life. Hot cocoa and whipped cream is more my jam, but Mom asked Brady to manage the beverages.

Great. Here come the Slaters.

Mr. and Mrs. Slater are both clutching bouquets of mini American flags to stick in people's yards. This makes more sense than the hot cocoa my mother is serving, seeing as how we're caroling on the 2nd of July. When I ask the Slaters for their song titles, Betty requests "The First Noel." Then Dale claims "Jingle Bell Rock." I tell him he's quite the rebel.

I just wish I could stop sweating.

Standing behind them is Natalie. She's dressed like Santa's helper. Little red dress. Green elf hat. Striped tights and laced-up boots. To complete the ensemble, she's carrying a pretend bag of gifts. She looks so innocent and cute. Why didn't I think of wearing something adorable like that? Since I had nothing else Christmas themed, I'm back in the extra-ugly sweater I borrowed from Tess. Emphasis on extra-ugly. And now, extra sweaty.

At the doorway, Natalie tells me she wants to sing Mariah Carey's "All I Want for Christmas is You." I tell her I'm not surprised. But I *am* surprised when she pulls a plate of brownies from her bag. The plate is wrapped in cellophane and tied with a big red bow. But still. Brownies? Seriously?

"I hope everyone loves walnuts!" she gushes. *Sure. With a side dose of Ex-Lax.* She's lucky no one else knows about her threat from years ago. She never actually gave me any brownies, and I never told a soul. That's because Natalie's a year younger than I am, and I didn't want her to think she had the upper hand. So I just played it cool and vowed never to eat any baked good she made. Ever.

At least tonight's brownies give me an excuse to leave my post at the front door before Beau steps up to name a song. I rush over to Brady and hand him the clipboard. "Tag, you're it. I've got to put Natalie's brownies in the kitchen." I almost shove the plate directly in the trash, but then I decide Natalie probably wouldn't sabotage everyone just to mess with me. To be sure, though, I'm going to steer clear of her brownies.

Almost as far as I'm steering clear of Beau Slater.

Before our departure, we all assemble outside. It's after seven o'clock, but it's also July, so the sun hasn't set yet. Mom does a head count while I swat at the flies buzzing around us. It almost feels like summer camp until Mom starts handing out the Santa hats and scarves she knitted.

(For the record, she's almost as bad at knitting scarves as Auntie Ann is at baking fruitcake.)

Aunt Remy, Mac, and the girls are all on board for carols. Big Mama's still not feeling herself, so she's staying back to rest. Auntie Mae and Uncle Cubby are at their house too. That's because their place is our last stop, so they offered to drive everybody home after. By then, we'll have probably run out of both mini flags and steam.

Our motley crew makes our way to Main Street first, where shops and restaurants are interspersed with private homes. We pass the Tipsy Tavern and Leo's Hardware. Then Hard Wear, the secondhand clothing store owned by Leo's wife, Betsy. Next to Betsy's place is Gracie's Glass Emporium, featuring both stained and handblown options.

"Kasey!" Mom calls out when we're approaching the first house. I'm walking near the front of the pack, so she's really making use of her outside voice. "Do you still have *The Official List of Carols*?"

"You mean since the last time you asked me? Yes, Mom." I flash her a thumbs up. "I'm still good."

She grins at me from the rear of our group where she's strolling next to Mr. and Mrs. Slater. Brady, Beau, and Natalie are behind me. Too close for comfort, if you want my opinion.

"Who's going first?" Natalie asks. "I'll volunteer if no one else wants to."

"Wow, Nat. That's so nice of you." *Yeah. What's your agenda?* "But we always start with the same song. It's tradition. Can you do 'O Come All Ye Faithful'? It's not Mariah Carey."

"No problem!" She climbs the porch steps and knocks on Evelyn and Hank Miller's door. The rest of us stay on the sidewalk, clutching our mini flags and cocoa mugs. Hank Miller opens the door and takes in the scene. Over his shoulder, he shouts for his wife.

"Evelyn! It's the carolers."

The fact that Hank is acting like this isn't odd tells you everything you need to know about Abieville. As soon as Evelyn joins Hank in the doorway, Natalie starts belting out "O Come all Ye Faithful." Apparently, now that she's all grown up, Nat Slater is plenty joyful and triumphant. After a few bars, the rest of us join in, achieving questionable pitches, tunes, and volumes.

In the middle of the second verse, Beau moves in close to me.

His voice is deep, and he hits most of the correct notes. When he bumps my shoulder, I turn, expecting to frown at him, but I'm struck by the scent of cinnamon and leather and something else that's purely Beau. Purely delicious.

Nope. Nopity nope.

He bumps me again, which can't be an accident, so I bump him back. Harder. Then I keep on singing extra terribly, exaggerating every one of my ohs and ahhs on purpose. I'm hoping Beau will think I'm weird and take a few steps back, but instead he winks at me. He actually WINKS!

Before I can begin to process what this means, Brady muscles his way in between us. My brother's voice is even more off-key than mine, which is pretty hard to accomplish. When the song ends, Hank and Evelyn disappear into their house without clapping.

Natalie turns back to the group. "I didn't think we were *that* bad."

"Maybe my 'O Holy Night' will go over better," Brady suggests. But then the Millers reappear in the doorway. Evelyn's carrying a tray of mini cupcakes with either red, white, or blue frosting. Hank's holding a bunch of 4th of July sparklers and a Bic lighter.

"That was wonderful," Evelyn announces. "And a bit strange. But mostly wonderful." Then she moves through our group, offering cupcakes, while Hank hands out sparklers, and lights them one by one.

My dad shrugs. "This is probably a fire hazard."

My mom shrugs back. "At least Ford's with us tonight."

Over the next two hours, we make our way up Main Street, past the cemetery, and across to Church Street. Then we head down to the houses on the lake, working through all the carols in our rotation. Brady ends up leading us in "O Holy Night" at least half a dozen times. I do "Jingle Bells" only once because I don't want Beau watching me more than is absolutely necessary.

Our group gets a few strange looks, but mostly smiles and

honks and waves from Abievillians who appreciate weirdness. By the time we reach Auntie Mae and Uncle Cubby's, most of us are pretty hoarse and all our sparklers are burned out.

Dale Slater shrugs. At least I think he shrugs, but it's hard to see now that it's gotten dark. "Did I hear someone say this would be our last stop?"

"Oh, my. Yes!" Betty blurts out. "I mean, OH MY! This has been fun!" Mom gets the hint and suggests we figure out who's going home with whom in which car.

Nella offers to drive a station wagon full of McCoys back to Big Mama's house. Auntie Ann, Uncle Irv, Ford, and Letty go with Three in his rebuilt Mustang. Auntie Mae says her two-door sedan fits four people comfortably. "I can take Betty, Dale, Elaine, and Phil."

"There are five of us," my dad points out.

She shrugs. "One of you has to be uncomfortable."

That leaves Nat and Brady—who claim the front of Uncle Cubby's pickup—and Beau and me, who get the back of his truck. *Great.* Before we leave, Mom suggests we take the long way around the lake. "That way we can see the boats lit up for the 4th of July!"

Why, universe? Why?

I make a move to climb over the tailgate first, but Beau is right behind me. "I'll give you a boost."

"I'm good," I say. Then my dumb flip flop slips on the metal, and I scrape my knee on the way down.

Beau puts his hands around my waist. "Please. Let me help." I turn around, expecting to frown at him again, but my traitorous body zings under his touch.

Why, body, why?

After I'm up, he hops into the truck far more gracefully than I ever could. I settle into the corner, crouching awkwardly, as far from Beau as I can get. Uncle Cubby revs the engine and leans out the driver's side window. "I'd like to get going someday," he calls out to us. "Are you two about done making out back there?"

My heart jolts. "Making out? Ha! We aren't making out! Why would you say we're making out?"

Beau nods at a pile of something next to me. The only light is coming from the porch, but I think it's a bunch of pillows and blankets. "Your uncle thinks we're making out back here because that's probably what he and your aunt do."

"Ewww." I cringe as the truck starts to rumble away, plunging us into darkness. And thank goodness for that, because I'm probably turning as red as Rudolph's nose. "Do not talk about Auntie Mae and Uncle Cubby making out!"

"What's the big deal?" Beau grins, and his teeth flash in the moonlight. "They're married. I think it's kind of cute."

"They're also kind of old. And they're definitely my aunt and uncle."

"Maybe so," Beau says. "But I kind of hope when I'm that old, I'll still be so in love with my wife that we take our truck to the lake to do a little kissing."

Now I bust out laughing. "A little kissing?"

"Sure." I catch the shadow of a head tilt. "A little of this and a little of that."

Oh no.

Now my imagination's off and running with a little of *this* and a little of *that*. Before I get to *the other thing*, my stomach fills with butterflies, every one of them flapping their wings. "What's wrong, Kasey?" Beau leans forward as the truck bumps over the road. "Are you jealous?"

"Ha! Of your future wife? Now that's a laugh. I feel nothing but pity for that woman, whoever she may be." Sinking back into the dark of the truck, I hope that Beau can't see me blush. We're quiet then for a while as my uncle takes the winding road around the lake.

I have to admit the scene is lovely. In honor of the 4th of July, most of the boats are strung with lights in red, white, and blue. Too bad Beau Slater's sitting next to me. He's totally ruining this festive moment. I try not to look at his face, but I can't help it.

The glow from the lights makes shadows along his jaw. Is he moving his lips? I can't tell if he's talking. Uncle Cubby's truck sure is loud.

"Did you say something?" I ask.

He leans in closer. "Can you hear me now?"

"Stop messing with me. What did you say?"

"What do you want me to say, Kasey Graham?"

Uncle Cubby takes a sharp turn, and out of nowhere, I'm knocked off balance. Thanks to my extra-awkward crouching, I fall directly onto Beau. He manages to catch me with one arm and hold us steady with the other. Wow. Grownup Beau is strong. I tip my chin until our noses are practically touching, and I can almost taste the peppermint on his breath. When his lips part—just a sliver—my heart begins to pound. The air is warm around us. The sky is filled with stars. Beau is staring at me in the moonlight, his gaze roaming my face. When my whole body starts to tremble, he must feel the shaking. Maybe he's waiting for my signal, letting me decide.

Slowly, ever so slowly, I find myself inching toward him. Closer and closer until his lips brush mine. Oh so soft. Oh so sweet. *Oh my stars.*

I'm kissing Beauregard Slater.

Like an explorer researching a map, he moves his mouth downward, gently feathering his lips along my jawline. He's blazing a trail of heat on my skin now, but it's his tenderness that sets me on fire. I'm so lost in the banging of my heart, I have to remind myself to breathe. But when I pause to suck in air, Beau breaks free from me.

"Kasey." He pulls away, darting his gaze up at the cabin of the truck. Why did he stop? His eyes are wide and expectant as he stares at the back window above us. But what exactly is he expecting?

A chill runs up my spine.

Beau must be setting me up again. Brady's probably about to open the window and pelt me with another bucket full of water balloons. How could I fall for their games again? They must think I'm so easy to play. Then. Now. Always.

The cold reality crashes over me. Beau isn't interested. I'll bet he only let our kiss happen so he could turn around and reject me. Now he can feel like he's come out on top once and for all. Beau Slater. The ultimate winner. He always wanted to beat me. Newspaper editor. Class president. Yearbook. Valedictorian. After all these years, I should've known better than anyone that Beau doesn't follow the rules. Heat floods my face, and I'm about to shove him away.

And that's when the gunshots start.

Chapter Seven

BEAU

Quick as a flash, I whip Kasey down and cover her whole body with mine. Not because I'm taking advantage of her. I'd never do that. My only goal is to protect her from whatever's shooting at us. So we're pressed against one another, and I feel her heart banging at my chest. But I don't have time to get scared, because out of nowhere another round of fireworks explodes. That's right. Fireworks. In the sky.

Yeah. Good job, dummy.

Kasey squirms underneath me. "Wait. Was that—what is happening?"

"I'm so sorry." I roll off her, shaking my head. "I thought for sure I heard bullets back there, but the village must be testing out the fireworks for the 4th."

Kasey props herself up on an elbow and stares at me. I can't blame her. I just made a huge fool of myself trying to save her. From fireworks. What an idiot.

"Are you all right?" I ask. "Did I crush you?"

She opens her mouth—that cherry red mouth—but before she can answer, the truck slows to a stop. We've arrived at the Grahams' house, and the car our parents are in pulls up next to us. I look up just in time to see Brady and Natalie in the front seat of the truck. They've been watching us through the back window. Watching me kiss Kasey. Busted.

Brady raps on the glass, probably practicing to knock my teeth out. Nat hops out first, and Brady follows her. They both come around to the back of the truck while I sit there next to Kasey, preparing to defend myself.

Brady slaps the side of the truck. "Are you two staying in there all night?" Kasey scrambles to the edge of the tailgate, and I climb out after her. I'm ready to take my lumps.

"Hey, man," Brady says. I cock my head, searching for signs of rage. But there's no stiff jaw. No murderous eyes. None of the warnings Brady sent when we were fifteen, and he caught me smiling at his sister. "Did you see the fireworks back there?" He grins. Just Brady being Brady.

"Yep. Sure did," I say. *Plenty of fireworks.*

I glance at Kasey, expecting her to ridicule me and tell everyone I thought there were gunshots, but she's not making eye contact. Oh man, kissing her was such a bad idea. For all the reasons.

Another round of fireworks goes off, and I duck. *Idiot.* My throat's still hot when my mom and Mrs. Graham approach.

"Wasn't that caroling so much fun?" asks Mrs. Graham.

My mother shoots me a look that says, *Do not answer honestly.*

"Fun." I nod. "Totally."

"Isn't that wonderful." My mother beams. "And since you're in the holiday spirit now, tomorrow should be even *more* fun." We all stare at my mom. "Didn't anyone tell you?" More staring from us. More beaming from my mom. "Elaine and I signed you kids up to judge the 4th of July floats. You know. For the *actual* holiday happening this week."

"Mrs. Slater." Brady clears his throat. "When you say *signed you kids up*, which kids do you mean, exactly?"

"Why all four of you, of course." My mother and Mrs. Graham exchange a pointed look. What's that about? "Elaine told me you'd all love to do it."

Brady turns to his mom. "No can do, *madre*. I've got work at the clinic."

Mrs. Graham frowns. "But you said you wouldn't have to work unless it was an emergency."

Brady's mouth goes crooked. "Oh, this is an emergency. *Believe* me."

Natalie chimes in next. "Sorry, Mom, but I've got plans too." She flashes a sugary sweet smile at me and Kasey. "Looks like you two out-of-towners will have to do the judging all by yourselves. Guess that'll teach you to stay away so long next time."

Brady chuckles. "Sounds fair to me." He and Natalie high five each other. Okay. Now I know for sure Brady didn't see me kissing Kasey. He's in way too good a mood.

You got away with it this time, Beau. Don't make that mistake again.

My parents say their goodbyes, then head toward their car. The Grahams thank us "young folk" for a great night and excuse themselves to go to bed. Brady turns to Nat, Kasey, and me. "I think the old folks still have a bunch of eggnog inside. And that stuff won't last until December. Someone's got to get through it. Who's in?"

Natalie raises her hand. "I am! And don't forget the brownies I made."

Brady turns to me "You coming with us, man?"

I glance at Kasey, who's shuffling her feet.

Keep away from her, Beau. Just start walking. You've got a job you love. An upcoming assignment others would kill for. You're living the dream. Sure, you don't have someone to share it with. But that's because you never wanted anyone besides Kasey. So let the rest of your success be enough. It has to be enough.

"I think I'll probably take off," I say. When Kasey doesn't argue, I paste a smile on my face to prove I'm all good. To her. To them. To myself.

Brady glances at the street. "Your parents left already. Need a ride?"

"Nah. It's a nice night." I stuff my hands in my pockets. "I'll walk, thanks."

He shrugs. "Suit yourself."

Kasey's eyes are trained on mine as I turn and walk away. I'm about two houses down the block when she calls out. "Hey, Beau. Wait up." She's not making this easy on me. Still, it's Kasey, so I reverse course to meet her halfway. When we reach each other, she stands there, looking up at me, and tucks a strand of hair behind her ear. Her hand is shaking. Did I do that to her?

Of course you did, Beau. This has to stop now.
Forever.

"About what went on with us back there in the truck," she begins. Then she squares her shoulders and her jaw. I scrub a hand over my face. I need to show Kasey I'm aware I blew it big time. That this can't go anywhere. For everyone's sake.

"I know. Kissing you was a big mistake." I have to grit my teeth to get the words out. "But don't worry. It won't happen again."

She swallows hard and looks at her feet.

See, Beau? Kasey's hurting because of you. This is exactly the kind of pain you've got to avoid from now on. You can't have her and keep your friendship with Brady.

When she lifts her head, her face is pale. "You better believe it was a mistake." She tips her chin, and her eyes flash. "And it definitely won't happen again."

Okay. Wow. I was way off again. Kasey's not in pain. She just totally despises me. "Try to keep your hands to yourself tomorrow," she blurts out. "Or else."

Without thinking, I cock my head. "Or else what?"

She takes a beat. Sputtering. "Or else … I don't know. Just stay away from me." She spins around and rushes back toward her house. I just stand there, watching her go.

My stomach's churning now, but at least I know the truth. After all these years, Kasey hasn't forgiven me. And instead of respecting her, giving her space, I jumped at the first chance to kiss her behind Brady's back. Literally. Behind my own sister's back too. What was I thinking?

I *wasn't* thinking. That's the quick answer. The longer one is I've been wanting to kiss Kasey like that ever since we were teenagers. But Brady made it clear from the start he didn't want me anywhere near his sister.

By the time graduation rolled around, I'd almost gotten used to burying my feelings for her. I'd done it for years. I figured I could make it through one more summer. After that, Kasey and I would be living on opposite sides of the country. Nothing left to hide, and no need to pretend anymore, right?

We couldn't be together then even if we wanted to.

So that's when I decided to apologize. To explain my pranks were just a disguise. That I'd only cooked up all the competition between us to keep her at a distance. I figured I had one last chance to be honest about my feelings. And more than anything, I hated thinking Kasey would leave for California hating me.

Which is why I bought her a charm bracelet.

Was it a corny gesture? Maybe. But I had zero game with girls, and only one girl I ever wanted. So I hid the bracelet in the pocket of my graduation robe, hoping to steal a moment with Kasey afterward. But the bracelet fell out while Brady and I were climbing into his car before the ceremony. The chain clattered into the gutter. Brady grabbed it before I could.

"What's this, man?" he asked. "You wearing jewelry now?"

"No way. I—" Heat flooded my face, and I had to think fast. "I only brought that stupid thing to mess with your sister. For getting valedictorian over me."

Brady narrowed his eyes even more. Did he doubt my story? I had to up the ante, so I glanced around like this was some big secret between us. "Do you want to help me set her up?"

A grin took over his face. Yeah. Brady was always on board for pranking Kasey.

I could've told him the truth. I could've punched him in his stupid, grinning face. Kasey didn't deserve this. She deserved better than me. Better than Brady.

Why did he have to make it so hard?

But I didn't have the guts to ask him that. Instead I let the guy run back into the house for a bucket and balloons. He came up with the rest of *our big plan*. The surprise attack. Him in the tree. Her down below. All those jerk moves that left Kasey soaking wet and hating me. Man, we were the worst to her.

No wonder she still can't stand me.

Looking back on that time now, I'll bet Brady knew the bracelet meant something more to me. That I had a different purpose in mind. But we were both just dumb kids then. Two boys figuring out how to be men and failing miserably. Acting tough. Fighting the world. A couple of wrecking balls who needed to grow up. The world took care of that over the years. But Kasey was smart to get away from me before then. Thousands of miles away.

She's got a whole new life I can't disrupt now.

I wrecked her back then. I won't do it again.

Chapter Eight

A TEXT THREAD WITH THE MCCOY COUSINS THE NEXT MORNING

Olivia: Hey, Kasey. I know we're trying to spend as much time together as possible this week, but I'm skipping the boat judging down at the lake and going back to bed. This is way too early to be awake on vacation, and the time difference is killing me. But I promise to show up a little later and get my tan on with you.
Darby: I won't make it to the lake either. I have to compose a strongly-worded email to my landlord. STAT. This could take a while. But I'll be at Aunt Elaine's place to make gingerbread houses this afternoon.
Tess: Uh oh. Why is your landlord on the receiving end of your wrath?
Darby: He's trying to increase our rent for the fall. By a lot. And it's too late to find another place now. He's got us over a barrel.
Mac: I can help you out with money, Darbs. No problem.
Darby: The fact that money isn't a problem IS the problem. Mr. Skinner found out we're the McCoys from McCoy Construction. Now he's jacking up his regular price. It's totally unfair. Places near the school are already ridiculously expensive.
Mac: Yeah. That's frustrating.
Darby: It's more than frustrating. It's infuriating. And the worst part is I can pay, but Hadley can't.

Mac: I'll cover your roommate's extra rent. I like Hadley.
Darby: Thanks. I already offered, but she won't go for it. She's got this thing about making her own way. It's admirable. But I know she won't budge.
Mac: She might not have a choice.
Darby: You haven't read my email.
Mac: Whoa. Now I'm scared of you.
Tess: Hey, Kasey. I think I'm going to stay here and keep Big Mama company, if it's okay with you. But I'll see you later for sure. #gingerbreadrules
Olivia: #gingerbreadisgross
Darby: Why aren't you back to sleep yet, Liv?
Olivia: Why aren't you emailing, Darbs?
Tess: For the record, we're all in separate rooms this time, Kasey. (LOL.)
Mac: It looks like Daisy and I are the only McCoys who are rallying this morning, Kase. We'll be over there soon so we can head to the lake together.
Tess: Kasey hasn't responded to anything on this thread so far.
Darby: Kasey? Are you there? You don't want to be late again. <skull emoji>
Olivia: Maybe she's still sleeping like a normal person.
Mac: I should have had at least one brother.

Chapter Nine

KASEY

Wow. You take one quick shower, and suddenly your phone blows up like a grenade. But not as bad as my heart exploded last night, thanks to Beauregard Slater. So I don't even respond to the texts from my cousins. I can't worry about Darby's roommate's rent. Or Tess's plans with Big Mama. Or Olivia's tan. Ugh. I'm too busy wallowing in my own humiliation.

Stupid, stupid, stupid.

How could I have been so incredibly stupid? I should've known from past experience—so much past experience—that I couldn't trust my heart around Beau. He made me believe he wanted to kiss me. He let me kiss him. I *was* kissing him. Then he pulled away like I was a hot potato he wanted to toss into someone else's lap. In the back of my Uncle Cubby's truck. Can a rejection get worse than that?

The answer is yes.

Because after we got dropped off, I still held onto some faint hope that Beau felt something when he kissed me too. Sure, I played it cool around Brady and Nat. I didn't want them getting any ideas about Beau and me until the two of us could talk. But when we finally were alone, what did he say? That kissing me was a big mistake. Won't happen again.

Great. Just great.

The thing is I didn't think he was pretending. For a breath of a moment, I actually believed Beau wanted that kiss as much as I did. Which means I'm still the fool, and he still has the upper hand. I felt like I was eighteen again, shivering in my brand new graduation dress. Hiding out at the docks after. It was a brutal flashback, except worse.

At least that day behind the gym, Beau stopped himself. But this time he let me put my lips on his. And I'd take being soaked by a bucketful of water balloons over knowing what his mouth tastes like, then having it stripped away.

Last night, in Beau's arms, I let my heart burst wide open. I could see our future stretched out before me. Days by his side. Nights holding hands. Me writing stories. Him taking pictures. We always had that in common. Companion goals, you know? When we were young, the competition made us enemies. But I thought *maybe* as adults, that kind of bond could cement us. For a split second, I allowed myself to believe we might make a legendary couple. The best team. Partners for life.

Joke's on you, Kasey!

Alone in my bedroom now, I swipe at fresh tears, remembering that summer after graduation. I never explained to my parents what happened. How Beau and Brady set me up. I felt like I couldn't. The truth was just too mortifying. The hurt so hot and sharp. But even though that old pain feels new again now, I refuse to hole up in my room like I did back then. The only one I'd be punishing this time is me.

And why? For letting Beau in? For thinking he might have feelings for me? Ha! At least I *have* feelings. Unlike Beau, who's apparently some kind of heartless robot. But now that I know better, I can protect myself. See these walls? They're thick and wide and tall. No one's getting through. Ever again. I won't let Beau Slater ruin one more minute of my life. I'll spend *all* my minutes proving I don't care.

Joke's on you, Beau!

"Kasey! Hurry up!" my mother shouts from the bottom of the stairs. "Betty wants the float judges down at the lake by nine o'clock!"

Ugh. Float judging with Beau Slater, maker of fools. (That's me. I'm the fool.)

"I'll be down soon!" I call out, but it sounds more like a choke.

"Mac and Daisy are going with you!" My mother pauses. Probably to turn down the Christmas music. "They're already here, Kasey!"

"Be right there!" I blow my nose, wipe a stray mascara streak, and toss the tissue in my Nicolas Cage trashcan. Sure, I'll paste on a smile, but my heart's clearly not up for float judging today. In fact, I feel more like the Grinch. Or whatever you'd call someone who hates the 4th of July.

A monster.

But I can't help it. I'm already way over celebrating Independence Day. I've spent twenty-three years as an independent woman. Do I really need to attend another party celebrating singleness? A nation busting out on its own? *Love the one you're with, Kasey Graham. That means you. Alone. Just you.*

As soon as Ms. Witherspoon hires me, I can forget all about relationships and jump headlong into work. I'll be the biggest success story in journalism. The youngest department head in history. Well, maybe not in history. But at *The Chronicle* for sure. Yes, once I get that call, I'll fly back to California, back to my real life. To a job that matters. Who needs love when you have a career, right, Kasey?

"KASEY!"

"Almost ready!" I take a deep breath and slip on a pair of red suede sandals that match my bright red sundress. This dress has pockets, so it's my favorite. Two quick spritzes of perfume. One last slick of cherry lip gloss. Fresh. Natural.

Go time.

*   *   *

Let the record show, I beat Beau to the docks. *See, Kasey? You're winning already.* Betty Slater is already there, posted up at a folding table by the first boat slip, so Beau must be coming separately. Whatever. I don't care. Okay. I care. A little. In fact, I feel kind of seasick looking at Mrs. Slater. So when Mac and Daisy stop to chat with her, I take advantage of the distraction to snag a judge's clipboard from the table without having to talk to her myself.

So far so good.

I just wish my stomach wasn't in a twist worrying that Beau might appear at any moment. It's not realistic to think I'll finish judging all the floats without running into him. What will he say when he sees me? And how will my body react? I'll probably break out in hives. Or blush myself to death. Maybe I should just shove him into the water.

Did I mention the floats are actually boats, and that the parade happens in the water? Yes. The floats literally float. That's how we do it here in Abieville. On the 4th of July, the people who aren't boat owners line up along the shore, across the bridge, and on the beaches. Then the people who *do* own boats ride around the lake, blasting patriotic music and cheering at the docks. Some Abieville boats get decked out with lights a week early. We saw those displays last night. But the real decorating—the stuff that gets judged—starts in the wee hours of the 3rd.

Why?

So the winner can be picked and ride in the first position of the water parade on the 4th. We call it the Boat Float Gloat.

And if you think there's not much anyone can do to decorate a boat, you'd be wrong. This town goes all out. Flags and banners. Ribbons and bows. Streamers. Blow up dolls. Even stuffed animals. No joke. Mr. And Mrs. Gootch's boat—the first one up for judging—has teddy bears dangling around the perimeter. Each bear is wearing a tiny uniform. Like old-time military stuff. An homage to Teddy Roosevelt? That's my best guess. It's been a long time since I took an American history class. All I know is each boat picks a theme, and this year's craziest has to be Auntie Mae and Uncle Cubby's.

Their boat looks like Santa's Village, and they've got Elvis Presley's "Blue Christmas" blasting over their sound system. Totally normal. Mac moseys up to their slip holding Daisy's hand. She's hopping along beside him, her crooked pigtails bouncing. Mac nods at our aunt and uncle's boat. "You can't pick theirs to win, right? That would be nepotism."

"Maybe." I shrug. "But it doesn't matter. My plan is to wait to see whichever float Beau picks, then vote for a different one."

"Huh?"

"Nothing." I look down at Daisy. "Hey there, little cuz. Do you like lollipops? Come with me."

Every inch of Margery and Glenn Wrightwood's boat that isn't under water is covered in red, white, and blue Tootsie Pops. How these boat owners manage to attach things to the sides without ruining the paint is a mystery. As we approach their boat, Daisy's eyes bug out. Margery comes down the ramp with a basketful of donuts. She's eyeing my judge's clipboard, so she's probably expecting to bribe me.

Along with getting to ride in the Boat Float Gloat position, the first place winner scores a free dinner at The Merry Cow. It's a highly-valued prize. And I'm not one for bribery, but I do love free donuts. So I take a cruller.

"Thanks, Mrs. Wrightwood."

"My pleasure, Kasey. Nice to see you back in town." She turns to Daisy. "Would you like a sucker?" Mrs. Wrightwood hands Daisy a blue Tootsie Pop.

"Tell the nice lady thank you," Mac says. But instead of speaking, Daisy bows. I'm starting to dig this little weirdo. She's *really* fitting in here.

As I make my way along the dock, the air is thick with the smells of different sunblock. Almost every boat owner is slurping down coffee after getting up to decorate well before dawn. I stop at each float, taking detailed notes and nibbling at my cruller. When my donut-scarfing and float-judging is almost at an end, I glance up and spot Beau a few slips down.

He's wearing red- and blue-striped swim shorts and a fitted white tank top. I can't help noticing the stretch of muscles underneath. Not to mention the swell of bare biceps. His hair's raked back from his bright eyes. In his hands he's carrying a judge's clipboard and ... is that an apple fritter? Good old Margery got to him too.

Mac follows my gaze to the end of the dock. "You all right?" he asks. Instead of answering, I consider bowing. But I'm not a silent four-year-old, so that would be too weird. Even for me.

"I'm fine," I say, widening my stance. Beau finally looks up and sees me. Ugh. As he starts strolling toward us, I remind myself I'm a strong, independent woman. Beau Slater did *not* get to me last night. Nope. I don't care about him. At all.

To make sure he knows this, when he reaches us, I frown. Extra big. Extra *I don't care*. "Apple fritter, huh," I say. "Take bribes much, Beau?" I lick my sticky lips to get rid of any traces of glaze on my mouth.

He squints at me, then lifts the hand holding his fritter up to block the sun. "I've got a sweet tooth. I couldn't say no."

"Ha! Really. Well. No is a hard word for *some* people to say."

Mac, who's standing between Beau and me, clears his throat. "Hey, Daisy. Let's you and me leave Kasey and Beau to their ... judging. I think I saw a stand selling cotton candy over by the Beachfront Inn." Mac darts one last glance my way. "I can't believe that old place is still hanging in there," he says. "You hang in there too."

Before I can beg Mac to stay as a much-needed buffer, he takes Daisy by the hand and walks her toward the oldest hotel on Abie Lake. I watch them go, wishing I could disappear into the beach crowd along with them. Instead, I'm stuck here with Beau. And a bunch of boat floats. And a churning stomach.

I turn to Beau, and he's still squinting. What's with that? "So." I square my shoulders. I'm trying to look unfazed. Cool as a cucumber. In a red dress. With a sticky face. "Have you seen all the boats yet?"

He ducks his head. "Pretty much."

"You have to see all of them, Beau. Those are the rules. Unless you don't care about rules."

He levels his gaze, then his eyes dip to my lips. "I care about a lot of things," he says.

My heart squeezes. "I'm sure you do." Too bad none of those things are me. Or my feelings. Or my dignity. Or—

"Kasey, I think we need to clear the air."

I want to scoff at him. I really do. But I'm pretty thrown off by his bright, squinty eyes. So I dig deep to muster my scoff. Ah. *There it is.* "I don't know about you, Beau, but my air is clear. Crystal clear."

His brows knit together. "Listen, Kasey. You don't have to like me ..."

"Good, because I don't."

"Nevertheless." He shifts his jaw. "Our mom's roped us into this judging thing, and we owe it to everyone to do our job and be fair."

I shrug. "I'm always fair. Sorry if you're not."

"I try my best. Sometimes life gets in the way of fair."

"I don't even know what that means." I sniff. "Anyway, let me see your clipboard."

He tilts his head. "Why?"

"I need to see which boat float you're picking to win."

He hides the clipboard behind his back. "Tell me yours first."

"No way. If I tell you which boat float I voted for, you'll just vote against my choice and ruin things. On purpose. Like you always do." I stomp my foot, but the show of temper makes me feel like Daisy. Who is four.

Beau's lip twitches. "Oh really. Is that what you think?" I swear on Santa Claus and George Washington, if Beau Slater laughs at me, I will shove him in the lake. "Well, *I think* that was actually *your* voting plan, Kasey. It takes a saboteur to predict sabotage."

"*Saboteur?*" I snort. "That's a pretty fancy word." Then I snort again. So it's a really good thing I am not trying to impress Beau Slater.

"You're a journalist," he says. "I thought you liked fancy words." Is he teasing me? He better not be teasing me. I tip my chin up. *Be strong, Kasey.*

"For your information, a good journalist never uses big words when a smaller word works better. But you're right. I am a journalist. In fact, I just nailed an interview for my absolute dream job at *The Chronicle*. And once I get that call from my new boss, I'm blowing this town and never coming back."

Beau's face clouds over. He likes it better when he's the only successful one between us. "I hope you hear from your boss soon," he says. His voice goes deep, almost gruff. "I want you to get your dream job."

"Huh. That would be a first." I grit my teeth. "Usually you steal the jobs I'm going after."

"Yeah." He averts his gaze. "Not this time."

"Because there's no competition anymore, right? My little newspaper can't possibly compete with your sainted photography work."

"Sainted ..." He studies me for a moment, then shakes his head. "I just take the assignments that are the farthest away from here. This may come as a surprise, Kasey, but you're not the only one who wanted out of Abieville."

"Good. Then we're agreed." A lump forms in my throat. Why do I even care that Beau's career is halfway across the world? We both have the same goal. To stay as far apart from one another as we can for the rest of our lives. So why has it been so hard for us to stay apart for the past few days? Since we got here, Beau and I have been stuck together for events beyond our control. There's always a plan. An excuse. Some reason. Every. Single. Day.

Hmm.

I wrinkle my nose. "Our mothers talk to each other a lot now, right?"

He shrugs. "I guess."

"And they're both well aware that I'm headed to LA next week, and you're headed overseas. They know our futures are elsewhere. So why have they been forcing us to be around one another all week?"

Beau furrows his brow. "What are you talking about?"

I start counting on my fingers because four-year-old Kasey is really coming out today. "One, my mom made sure she and Brady left the room so you and I were alone that first night with the poster. Two, my mom invited your family for caroling, and once she saw us in the truck together after, she suggested we take the long way around the lake. Three, your mom signed us up for float judging today. When have we ever done *that* before? Four, my mom planned gingerbread decorating after we're done here. Five, your mom invited us all over for fireworks tomorrow night." I hold up my completely opened hand, all fingers up, plus a thumb. "My mom. Your mom. Both our moms. They're in on it. *Saboteurs.*"

"I don't know, Kasey. That sounds a little far-fetched." He runs a hand through his hair and it practically sticks up straight. I wish he didn't look adorable.

"It's not far. Or fetched. It makes perfect sense. Neither of our moms wants us to leave town. They want to keep us here in Abieville. Together. Think about it. Haven't they both been all mushy about having their babies home?"

Beau nods, but not in agreement. More like he thinks I'm nuts. "Wanting your kids around is kind of normal, isn't it?"

"My mom?" I squawk. "Normal?"

"Well." He chuckles. "You've got a point there."

"I've also got a plan." I scan my clipboard. "Okay. Here's the deal. I'm voting for Margery and Glenn Wrightwood to win the boat float decorating contest. Their donuts were delicious."

He looks down at his fritter. How has he not eaten that thing yet? "I think your aunt and uncle should win," he says. "Christmas is way more original than fritters and Tootsie pops."

"Fine." I check the box for Auntie Mae and Uncle Cubby's entry with my trusty Sharpie. "As long as it's your idea, no one can accuse me of favoritism." I hand him my clipboard and stick the Sharpie in my pocket. I really do love a sundress with pockets.

Beau looks down at my clipboard. "What am I supposed to do with this?"

"Go turn in our ballots. I've got something to do first." I slip my phone from my other pocket and make a call while Beau looks on. Fine. I don't care if he hears what I'm about to say.

My mother answers on the third ring. "Kasey!" She always sounds like a giant ball being shot from a cannon. "How are things going there? I'm just getting the supplies ready for the gingerbread houses over here."

"That's why I called, Mom."

"We've got frosting and candy canes and M&Ms, of course. Plus licorice and those teeny tiny peppermints. Can you think of anything else we might need? Maybe on the way back from the lake, you and Beau could stop by the mini mart for—"

"No, Beau and I can't do that, Mom. And just so you and Mrs. Slater know, your plan isn't going to work."

There's a long pause. More silence than my mother's managed since I've been home. Or maybe ever. "You sound upset," she says. The guilty can sound so innocent when they want to. "What's wrong, dear?"

"I think you know what's wrong." I glance at Beau, who's shaking his head. Sure, my heart skips a beat at his cuteness, but I'm only on his side when it comes to our mothers. It's not like we're a team. We just have a common enemy now.

"Kasey Elizabeth," my mother says. "I don't have time to guess what's going on with you. I still need to stop by Auntie Ann's to pick up the sheets of gingerbread before everyone gets here. She's got walls and ceilings and floors of gingerbread to assemble. Enough for two dozen houses."

"Why can't Auntie Ann bring the gingerbread when she comes over?"

"Well." There's another pause, and I can practically see the wheels spinning in her brain. "You make an excellent point. But the rest of your attitude has been very strange today."

"Oh, I'm plenty strange, Mom." When Beau nods at this—in agreement this time—I try to kick his shin, but I almost fall in the lake. So Beau has to snatch me back up onto the dock. My elbow tingles where his hand grips my skin. Then the rest of my arm erupts in goosebumps. When he hauls me in close to steady me, my whole body shivers. Stupid, traitorous body.

So much for dignity.

"Kasey?" my mother pipes up. "Are you still there?"

I step away from Beau, to catch my breath. "Yes, I'm here. With Beau. We're onto you and Betty Slater, and we're not playing along anymore." Speaking for both of us gives me almost as much of a thrill as Beau's warm touch. "This means we are *not* coming over for gingerbread. Instead, we are going to ...ummm ..."

I dart my eyes at Beau and let the sentence dangle there unfinished because I've somehow gotten myself into a situation where I'm stuck with Beau again. His eyes go wide. Expectant. He's waiting to hear what's next for us too.

"Kasey? What happened?" my mom asks. "I think you cut out on me." She smacks the phone. "You and Beau are going to what?"

Chapter Ten

BEAU

"So. Where to, Captain?" I glance at Kasey, who's sitting shotgun in my dad's truck. She's got the window rolled down, and her red hair's flying. She's kicked off her sandals, and her bare feet are on the dashboard. Man, this girl's adorable. Correction. This *woman* is *beautiful*. And she might be acting a little crazy right now, but crazy suits her. Still, I need to remember I can't be looking at Brady's sister through this particular filter. You know. The one where all I see is how much I want to kiss her. Again.

"Let's go to the school," she says.

My gut clenches. "Really?" I take a beat. Then I take another. "The last time we were there ... was pretty messed up."

"Yeah. You're telling me." She gazes out the windshield, which is streaked with dirt. If I'd known she'd end up with me in this truck, I would've washed the glass this morning. In fact, I would've polished every inch of this old clunker. I just want to take care of Kasey. Make things right with her.

"The thing is," I say as gently as I can, "I don't think going by the school's such a great idea."

She keeps her focus on the road in front of us. "You owe me, Beau." Well. She's got me there. I can't say no. Or maybe I don't want to.

Before long, we're rounding the east side of the lake, on our way toward the cemetery. Our destination is a few blocks up, beyond a stretch of moss-covered tombstones. Brady and I used to play hide and seek here, accusing each other of being scared. To me the ghosts at the school are worse, so I'm driving extra slow on purpose.

Just past the cemetery, I turn into the school's parking lot. Somebody's raked all the fallen leaves into piles along the curb. Even though the stone buildings are empty now, I can taste the thousands of bologna sandwiches I ate in the cafeteria. I pull up and park. Before I've even shut off the engine, Kasey's out of her seatbelt, hopping down from the truck and slamming the door.

She pokes her head in through the open window. "Follow me."

"Hold on a minute," I say. But she doesn't hold on a minute. She takes off at a run. "The concrete's got to be hot," I call out. "You want your sandals?" She's either too far gone to hear, or she's intentionally ignoring me. Either way, I collect her sandals from the floor of the truck to bring with me. I may not be able to kiss Kasey Graham, but I can make sure she doesn't burn her feet. In fact, if she'd let me—and Brady wouldn't object—I'd take care of that crazy, beautiful woman for the rest of my life.

Get real, Beau. Kasey hates you. And talking to yourself won't change that. So you can't love her.

But what if I do?

Beau. Just stop.

I make my way around the front of the school, but Kasey's out of sight. I know where she went.

And I wish I didn't. As I head toward the gym, my stomach twists, and it keeps on twisting the closer I get to the spot where I broke Kasey. Not her heart. Kasey wasn't in love with me back then. And now she never will be. But I sure broke her spirit that day. I'd promised her a peace-offering. At the very least, she must've expected I'd treat her kindly. Instead, Brady and I humiliated her. And for that I'll never forgive myself.

Clearly, she hasn't forgiven me either.

I wanted to apologize to her back then, but she steered clear of me the rest of the summer. I never ran into her around town, and whenever I was at her house, Kasey stayed in her room. Of course I couldn't talk to her in there. Not with Brady around.

But Brady's not around now.

When I come around the back of the gym, my insides are already on fire. And then I see Kasey, standing under the same cluster of trees where I almost kissed her. My pace slows. It's been more than five years, but I can still picture Brady hiding above us in the top branches.

"Hey, there." I choke out the words. She's so beautiful, but her eyes flash a warning. So I duck my head and set her sandals on the ground a few feet away from her.

"I figured you'd find me here." She pulls her phone from her pocket. She messes with the screen for a moment then she holds up the phone, turned sideways like you'd do for a video.

"What's going on, Kasey?"

She fixes me with a stare. "I want you to confess," she says. "Admit out loud what you and my brother did to me after graduation."

"I can't." I shake my head as pangs of guilt claw their way up my throat. "Not on camera."

"I need you to do this, Beau. For closure." She swallows hard. "Don't you think you owe me that much?"

I rub a hand across my chin, considering my options. I could refuse. Be stubborn and stand up to her. *Or.* I could let down my guard like she did that day. She was so vulnerable, looking up at me, with hope and trust in her eyes. She'd been wrong to trust me then. But I want her to know she can trust me now. And she's right. I do owe her this.

I'll do what she asks.

"All right." I shift my jaw and unclench my teeth. "If that's what you want."

"Good." A slow smile spreads across her face. Like she can't believe I'm agreeing to do this. "Give me one second to hit record, then you can start." She presses a button and aims the phone's camera at me again.

"Okay. Here goes." I take a deep breath, blow it out. "Five years ago, after graduation, I asked Kasey to meet me here, behind the gym. I told her I had something to give her and even though she had no reason to believe me—not after all the different ways I'd messed with her—she showed up anyway." My chest aches as I say this.

What a supreme jerk, Beau.

"I let her think my reasons were legitimate, but Brady was waiting up in those trees." I glance up at the highest branches. The sun's peeking through now, light streaking down on Kasey.

She nods. "Don't stop, Beau. You're just getting to the good part."

My mouth's dry as a dust bowl, and a bead of sweat rolls off my brow. "The thing is," I say to the camera, "I knew Brady was up there, watching us, but I couldn't help myself. I moved in for a kiss. That wasn't part of the plan." I take a beat, and Kasey makes a small noise in the back of her throat. This story can't be easy for her to hear, but she might as well know the truth. "Anyway, before anything happened between us—before I got to kiss Kasey—Brady took matters into his own hands ..."

Kasey's jaw goes tight. "Tell everyone what Brady did, Beau. What you *let* him do."

"He started pelting her with water balloons. A whole bucket full of them. The water must've been freezing, but Kasey barely flinched. She just stood there taking it, getting wetter and wetter. I think her strength made Brady even madder. And he was probably already mad at me for almost kissing his sister ..." My voice trails off.

"Then what happened?" she prompts.

"Brady was in the tree cracking up, and I stood there feeling like the world's worst human. I *was* the worst for letting Brady hurt her."

Kasey flips her phone around and says, "The end." She taps at her screen. But I wasn't done yet. She looks up from her phone and rubs at her nose with a fist. Is she fighting back tears? My stomach sinks even deeper into the pit of shame inside me.

"Kasey." I take a step toward her, but she backs away.

"That last part's not entirely true, is it? The part where you said you let Brady hurt me. *You* hurt me. *You* did, Beau. You need to own your part."

"You're right," I nod. "And I wanted to explain things to you back then. I would've apologized, but you ran off. And then we both left for school." I take another step toward her, but she steps back again. "So I'm telling you now. From the bottom of my heart. I'm truly sorry I hurt you. I know I hurt you over and over. But I'm not that stupid kid anymore."

She blinks, hard and fast, shaking her shoulders like she's shaking off my apology. Then she starts back in on her phone, tapping away. She looks up at me. "All right, Beau. I just forwarded the video confession to your phone. Now there's just one more thing I need you to do for me."

I cock my head. A question. What does she want me to do?

"Send it to your mom," she says. "Then to mine."

My throat constricts like I'm being strangled by a boa constrictor. "But ... why?"

Kasey shifts her weight. Is she feeling unsure? Or just thrown off balance, caught up in the memory? Either way, I want to make things better for her. Still, my chest burns, imagining anyone else finding out what Brady and I did. Especially our mothers.

"If they know what happened with us back then," Kasey says, "they'll stop trying to make something happen between us now." Her lips tremble. A terrible shake. "Maybe they thought it was a brilliant idea to push us together this week, but they don't know the real you, do they?"

"Maybe you don't know me either," I say, my eyes locked on hers. Kasey blinks, but the set to her mouth says she's not budging. I glance at her phone then meet her gaze again. "Even if I wanted to, I can't send that video to anyone because I don't have my phone with me."

She takes a beat, furrows her brow. "Fine." She unlocks the screen on her phone and hands it over. "Use mine."

"All right, Kasey." I bob my head. "I can do that. If this is really what you want." She nods. A tight, quick one. "Okay," I say. But instead of sending a text, I open up her camera app, switch the setting to video, and flip the lens back at me. *Take a breath now, man. It's time to say your piece.*

"Hey, there, Kasey Graham. It's me. Beau Slater. I've been an idiot. I've always been an idiot, but not the way you think. I didn't actually set out to torment you back in high school. Not at first. I was just a fifteen-year-old kid who had the misfortune of falling for his best friend's sister. That would be you, Kasey. And yeah, I should've told Brady how I felt. I should've told you. Instead I told myself it was guy-code. You don't date your friend's little sister, right? No way. Never. So I did everything I could to push you away."

When I take a breath, Kasey jumps in. "So you're blaming my brother now?"

Guess we're in interview mode. But I keep the camera aimed at me. "No, it was my fault. And I can accept that. The truth is Brady didn't even know how I felt about you. Or maybe he did. Maybe that's why he worked so hard to mess with you too. It's not an excuse. Just the truth. I—"

"Stop!" She puts a hand up.

"Not before I tell you I really *did* have something to give you that day. A charm bracelet. Twenty-four karat gold. I bought it at Murphy's Jewelers."

She shifts her jaw, but she says nothing.

"After the way Brady and I had been treating you, I got the idea to give you the bracelet as an apology."

Kasey's shoulders begin to quake. "Why on earth should I believe you now?" Her voice is a quiet tremor.

"Ask Pat Murphy. He'll tell you."

She presses her lips together like she's trying not to lose control. "So after years of pranking me, you were just going to give me ... a bracelet?"

"Yeah." I flinch. "I knew it was a long shot. And I was afraid you might laugh in my face, but I was also hoping somewhere deep down, you had feelings for me too." Kasey's eyes are shining now. She looks down at her bare feet. "Anyway," I say. "That was my plan but ..." I let the story trail off. She knows how it ends.

I stop recording, and Kasey lifts her face. Her beautiful face.

"Beau." Her voice is almost a whisper. "I can't believe I'm saying this, but I think you might be telling the truth."

I move toward her again, and this time she stays put. Sweat's rolling down my back, but Kasey's shivering in her dress. I want to wrap my arms around her to stop the tremble. But whatever happens between us now needs to be on her terms. I take another step forward. Then I reach out and poke the bare skin of her shoulder.

"Tag." I say. "You're it."

She blinks. Bends her head. "I don't get it."

"You're in charge now, Kasey." I hold up her phone. "Say the word, and I'll send these videos to everyone in town. I'll stay away from you for the rest of this week. Or I'll stay with you for the rest of this week." I move another inch closer. Close enough to feel her shudder without even touching her. "Whatever you want," I say. "Anything for you." My words are raw and jagged, and I'm sure she can hear my heart pounding. It's banging that loud. But I don't care. I'm done pretending.

Kasey lifts her face to mine, and I feel her breath come warm and quick. In this moment, I'd do anything to kiss this woman. Quit my job. Give up my best friend.

Say the word and I'm yours, Kasey Graham.

"What do you want?" I whisper.

She parts her lips. "I want revenge."

Chapter Eleven

KASEY

"Revenge?" Beau's staring down at me, his eyes wide with disbelief. "*That's* what you want?"

No. What I *really* want is to kiss him. And I also want to believe him. So very badly. I told Beau I *thought* he might be telling me the truth even before I was completely sure. Now I'm afraid if I let my guard down, my lips will start doing things my heart's not ready to back up. So for my own good, I should pull away. Too bad my body wants us to stay this close for the rest of my natural-born life.

"I guess revenge might be too strong a word," I say, taking a step back and blinking fast. "How about payback? No. That's still not quite right." I shake my head. "I've just been on the receiving end of a few too many pranks over the years. Is it so wrong to want to give everyone else a little taste of their own medicine?"

"Okay, Kasey. You win." His shoulders sag, and he takes another step away from me. This doesn't feel like winning at all. "What kind of medicine did you have in mind?"

I chew my lip, already regretting going down this path. But payback is safer than kissing, right? Way safer. "I haven't figured out all the details yet," I say. "But maybe we could teach our moms a lesson about trying to manipulate us. And maybe not just our moms. Maybe Brady too. And Natalie."

"Huh." Beau furrows his brow. "What does Nat have to do with this?"

"Do you seriously not know?"

"Know what?" Based on the tilt of his head, he isn't kidding.

"I never did anything to Natalie, but your little sister sure hated me anyway. She even threatened to secretly slip Ex-Lax into my brownies once."

"Whoa." Beau shakes his head. "I guess Nat wanted to keep us away from each other as much as Brady did. She must've figured out I had feelings for you too." At this, my heart skips a beat, and those darn butterflies rush back to my stomach. Why is Beau saying things like this to me? *I had feelings for you.* Then again, he used the past tense.

Had.

As terrible as that word feels—sinking inside me—it also makes complete sense, and reminds me why I can't let myself fall for Beau Slater any more than I already have. He can't afford to care about me now. He's got a globe-trotting career to pursue, and he won't give up his dream job. He can't. And I get it. He's wanted to be a photographer since high school, just like I dreamed of being a journalist.

Suddenly, my cheeks flush pink, and I remember Beau wasn't the only one of us who took something from the other back then. "I owe you an apology, too, Beau."

"Well. This is unexpected." He raises an eyebrow. "But I guess you're all about teaching lessons now. So I should learn to expect the unexpected from you." He takes a beat. "What do you have to be sorry about?"

I swallow. Hard. If I had a collar to tug, I would. "I stole the job of yearbook editor right out from under you. And I knew how much you wanted it."

"Ooooh, yeah." He blows out a long, exaggerated breath, like I just socked him in the belly. "That *was* pretty rough, Graham.

And I was definitely disappointed, so I'll accept your apology. But I always figured you only did that because I went after editor of the paper. I drew first blood."

"You did. That's true." A cloud passes over the sun, and I suck in a hot breath. The air is still thick and humid. "But you know the old saying. Two wrongs don't make a right."

He scrubs a hand over his chestnut hair, and in that moment, I don't care about wrongs or rights, I just want to be those fingers in the waves. I want to sit in the shade of this pine tree and kiss Beau Slater. Forever.

"Here's the thing, though," he says. Then he lays a palm on my shoulder, and a hot shiver runs up my spine. Extra-high voltage. "Doesn't the whole *two wrongs don't make a right* idea go against your little revenge plot?"

Ugh. "I hate it when you've got a good point," I groan. "Could you ease up on that please?"

"I'll try." He chuckles and drops his hand. "But reining in *all* my good points might take some work. I'm pretty much full of good points, you know."

I puff out a laugh. "Oh, you're full of something all right." When his eyes dance, my pulse races even faster. It's *possible* I want to hatch a plot with Beau just so we have an excuse to be together without me having to admit my heart is begging for it. "Okay." I nod. "Let's agree we won't do anything overtly mean. Nothing involving laxatives or water balloons." I lift a brow. "But we can still have a little fun with everyone."

"What kind of fun, exactly?"

"Well." I tilt my head. "Our moms have obviously been throwing us together all week, thinking we wouldn't notice what they're doing."

Beau raises a hand. "In their defense"—he chuckles again—"I didn't notice."

"Yeah. Well." *There's plenty you don't notice. Like the effect you're having on me now.* I avert my eyes. This next part I can't say while looking directly at Beau. "If our moms want us to be a couple so bad, we could always pretend we are. A couple, I mean. We can act like they were right all along, just to mess with them."

As I say the words, my insides get warm. Really warm. Like apple-pie warm. I'll have to be careful not to enjoy this role too much. Because it will be just an act. An act with an end date. I lift my gaze, and Beau's eyes bore right through me.

"All right." His voice has gone gravelly, and my whole body floods with heat. He's actually agreeing? "When and how do you want to do this?" he asks.

"Hmm." *Think, Kasey. Think!* "You know my family is invited to your house to watch the fireworks show tomorrow. So maybe, while we're all there together, you and I could put on a show of our own." I pause, waiting for Beau to object to the specifics. But he doesn't, so I keep going. "We can lay it on super thick. Like holding hands and snuggling up to one another." I inhale. Exhale. "We'll fake being in love."

"I can do that," Beau rasps. Then he clears his throat. I'll miss that gravel. "But our moms aren't stupid," he says. "Do you think they'll buy it?"

I *think* I don't care. I *think* I want to do it anyway. But instead of admitting that, I offer him a small smile. "I can be a pretty good actress when I want to be." This is truer than Beau needs to know. For instance, right now I'm doing a great job of pretending my knees aren't weak just smelling his cologne. And noting the curve of his lips. Seeing the cords of his neck flex. Watching his muscles strain under his shirt.

"I'll bet," he says. Then he folds his arms across his chest, and oh, wow. There go those muscles again. I shift my gaze and focus on his Adam's apple. Beau's nice, neutral Adam's apple. Nothing sexy about that. Except every time he swallows, I kind of want to kiss him in that exact spot.

But back to my strategy.

"In the meantime," I say, "and for the exact opposite reason, Brady and Natalie will go nuts if they think we're together. They'll completely freak out." I lift a finger, like Watson about to reveal the answer to Sherlock Holmes. "And that's when you and I will hit everyone with the truth."

He stares at me. "Which is what?"

"That there's absolutely nothing going on between us."

"Right. Absolutely nothing." He squeezes his arms even tighter, and it's like he's squeezing all the breath out of me at the same time. "So what's your end game, Kasey?"

I square my shoulders. "What do you mean?" He can't possibly know that—deep down—my end game might be an excuse to be close to him. An excuse that comes with an escape clause.

"I mean, what are you hoping to accomplish?" he asks. "What are *we* hoping for?"

Gulp. Oh that. "I guess I'm hoping my mom will learn she can't fool me. Or control me. Or whatever."

"Okay." He nods. "But what will Brady and Nat learn?"

I huff out a laugh. "That *we* pranked *them*." I'm expecting to feel triumphant, but my stomach's more hollow than anything else. I spent half my life resenting being Brady's doormat. What if I'm swinging the pendulum too far in the opposite direction? Still, I don't want to think about that right now. I just want to focus on being close to Beau for one night. Even if it's pretend. Even if it's brief. That's still better than nothing.

He rubs at the back of his neck. "And after everyone finds out the truth, you and I will go back to being absolutely nothing to one another. Do I have that right?"

This stops my heart for a beat. "I mean, yes. I'll be in LA, and you'll be traveling the world. We'll both be living our dream lives, finally doing what we've always worked for."

"Makes sense." Beau meets my gaze, and something flashes behind his eyes.

"You *do* like your job, don't you?"

"No." He drops his chin. "I don't like my job. I *love* it." His voice is thick, and I can practically *see* the word "love" on his lips.

"That's great." I swallow. "Then we're both going to be happy after all." Even as I say this, my insides churn. A part of me was hoping Beau would fight for the possibility of *us*. But I shouldn't hope for something that wouldn't be good for him. He looks down at me, and I tip my chin up. I'm a giant bowl of ache. Before he can see my true thoughts, I bend over to pick up the sandals he brought me from the car.

"Thanks for these, by the way." I brush the dirt from the bottoms of my feet and slip the sandals on.

"Least I could do." He dips his head, shy and sweet, then he hands me my phone. "So. Are we sending these videos?"

I swallow hard and force my mouth into a crooked tilt. "Mmm ... not yet. But I *am* going to hold onto them in case you back out tomorrow night. Or if you do a horrible job of pretending I'm the love of your life."

"I'll do my best." Beau half-smiles, and my stomach swoops.

"You better." I poke his chest. Oof. That rock-hard chest. "I'm counting on you to convince everyone you think I'm the bee's knees. If not, I'll post this video of you confessing all over the place."

"Hold up." His lips twitch. Oh, how I love when they do that. "Did I just hear you describe yourself as the bee's knees?"

I snort. Oh, how I hate it when I do that. "I'm just helping you out, giving you more reasons to be fake-in-love with me. I mean, who can resist a woman this cool?" I sweep a hand down my body, and his eyes trace the path. Why did I draw attention to myself like that?

"You *are* the coolest, Kasey Graham."

"Why, thank you, Beauregard Slater. That might be the smartest thing you've ever said."

* * *

By the time Beau drops me off at my parents' house, most of my extended family is already gone, but Mac and Daisy are still sitting in the front room along with half a dozen freshly decorated gingerbread houses. My dad's favorite holiday album is playing. John Denver is singing "Christmas for Cowboys." One glance at Daisy's sticky face tells me my littlest cousin has had more than her fair share of candy today.

"Hey there, Cuz," I say. Mac's wiping Daisy's mouth with a damp paper towel. He stops wiping and looks up at me.

"Well, well, well. The prodigal daughter returns." He raises one eyebrow. "Where've you been all afternoon?"

"Places." I kick off my sandals and collapse on the couch next to Daisy.

Mac nods in the direction of the kitchen. Based on the laughter coming from the other room, Aunt Remy and the triplets are still in there with my mom. "*Some* people might require a more specific answer than that," he says.

I cringe. *Uh oh*. My stomach twists. By skipping the decorating, I missed a chance to spend more time with Darby, Liv, and Tess. Luckily, I have plenty of chances to make up for it before the week is over. We've still got the A-Fair. And the parade. Our family's Christmas Eve and Christmas. "I hope no one's too upset," I say softly.

"Nah. We all had a great time." Mac wads up the paper towel and sets it on the coffee table. "But be warned. Your whereabouts have been the subject of quite a bit of speculation this afternoon." He offers me a sly smile. "Were you at least having fun?"

I glance at the kitchen again. "I've been busy. Let's just leave it at that."

Mac's sly smile spreads into a full-blown grin. "Well, I for one am really glad I got to see you today. So is Daisy. Although she's mostly showing her enthusiasm by eating her weight in sugar."

"Thanks, Mac." I smile back at him. "For the record, I'm glad I got to see you both too." I reach out to scoop Daisy onto my lap, and I'm a little surprised when she lets me. As she settles back in my arms, I smell gingerbread sugar and peppermint. "What do you think, Daisy? Did you have fun today?" She says nothing, just sticks a thumb in her mouth. I decide this response means *yes*.

Daisy might not be talking, but that doesn't mean she can't communicate.

"There you are, Kasey!" My mother bursts into the room. She's wearing a hat made of pretend deer horns, just like the scene from *How the Grinch Stole Christmas*. You know the one—when the Grinch makes his dog, Max, wear reindeer antlers. "We were so worried." She's actually wringing her hands, and I feel a stab of guilt about our plans to deceive her.

"I'm fine, Mom."

She splays her hands to indicate the display of gingerbread houses. "You missed all the decorating. Who knows the next time everyone will be together for this again."

Another stab of guilt cuts through me. "I'm sorry. I wasn't thinking."

Daisy crawls off my lap and starts picking M&Ms off the nearest gingerbread house.

"We lost track of time today," I add, "but it won't happen again."

"We?" My mother adjusts her antlers. "Who's *we*?"

I gulp. "Just me, myself, and I."

"Humph." She lets her hands fall at her sides. "You know, this is just like that time you disappeared after graduation, Kasey. No reasons. No explanation. Just gone. Poof."

Ugh. My stabs of guilt shift to a sick pit in my stomach. "I really am sorry, Mom."

"Sorry or not, we can't get back our time today now, can we?"

"No, ma'am. We can't."

Mac stands, lifting Daisy up onto his shoulders. "I think we're gonna head back over to Big Mama's. You hang in there, Kase." I gaze up at my cousin and find myself blinking back tears.

"Thanks, Mac. You too."

My mother walks him and Daisy to the door, then she turns back toward me. "Aunt Remy and the girls were about to leave too. You should say hi before they go. And Kasey? Try to stick around tomorrow." When she heads back into the kitchen, I hear her muttering.

We lost track of time.

As much as the memory hurts, I'm grateful my mom brought up graduation. It's a reminder of why I absolutely can't have feelings for Beau. No matter how much I may want to.

No matter what kinds of tricks my heart keeps playing.

Chapter Twelve

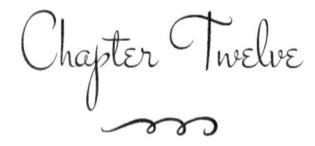

BEAU

"You've got this, Beau. You do. Come on now. Get a grip." Yep, that's me. Pacing in circles and pep-talking myself. Mom's out back arranging lanterns on the deck. Natalie's in her room doing whatever she does to get ready. Dad's setting up folding chairs and filling up coolers. That just leaves me taking another lap around the room.

Kasey texted to say her family will be here by 8:00 for the fireworks. I check my watch, then check my reflection in the mirror. I barely recognize myself. Is this the Beau who's been on safaris and in submarines? Oil rigs and front lines? For a guy who tries to live authentically, I'm pretty shocked Kasey got me on board with her scheme.

She *thinks* I agreed to pretend I'm in love with her. But the truth is I *am* in love with her. This is the opposite of what I did in high school—crushing on her hard, but acting like her enemy. I'm not even sure how this new plan goes. I've never faked something I actually felt before. All I know is the minute I started putting myself out there yesterday, Kasey pumped the brakes.

I'd been this close to admitting how I *authentically* feel. Heart in my hand, tongue tied in my mouth. I wanted to kiss her, but first I asked what *she* wanted. Then she looked up at me with those big blue eyes of hers ...

... and said *revenge*.

Yeah. That ripped the rug right out from under me. I was offering her Beau, and she picked payback. But I get it. We were terrible to her back then. That's why I'm willing to help her now, even though deception flies in the face of everything I am as a grown man. Still, as far as deception goes, this plan is pretty harmless. Plus it's how I actually feel. I really do care about Kasey. So I'm not really deceiving anyone. Except myself.

I should get a gold star for rationalization.

On the bright side, I don't think Kasey hates me anymore. For a moment yesterday, I even let myself think something might be happening between us. I could've sworn her heart was stirring too. And maybe if she knew how I truly felt, she might be swayed. But before I could tell her, she brought up the whole job thing. Told me work is more important. My work. Her work. We'd never work as a couple, because of our work.

I mean, of course Kasey's job is a big deal. She's waited five years for this break. As for me, not everyone gets the chance to work with a Pulitzer-Prize winner. The truth is, doors are opening for us and we'd probably be stupid to shut them. Still, I'm going to take a chance tonight and shoot my shot. When the moment is right, I'm going to tell Kasey what I want. Her. And if she turns me down, I'll step back. Let her go.

At least that way, I'm the only one who's losing.

There's a fumbling at the door, and Kasey's mother pokes her head in. "Knock, knock, knock," she says, coming inside. She's carrying a plate of snickerdoodles and wearing a green and red cardigan covered in Santa Clauses. She's a walking Hallmark movie. Very yuletide. Very Elaine Graham.

Kasey is behind her, looking more gorgeous than ever. She's dressed in white, like some kind of holiday angel. Her hair is loose around her face. I want to reach out and touch those waves, gather them together, breathe her in. And tonight I can, right? Since we're *pretending* to be a thing.

Mrs. Graham sets the cookies on the dining room table, and Kasey sets her phone down next to it. Is that supposed to be some kind of warning to me? A reminder that she's still got the videos if I don't follow through?

Well. Don't worry, Kasey Graham. I intend to follow through.

As if she heard my thoughts, she glances up and meets my gaze. Then she winks at me. Huh. Is that a signal? We didn't talk this plan through in detail, so I'm not sure when to start our show.

I'm waiting for some cue when my mom comes in from the yard. She's got on a red- and white-striped top and blue pants with white stars. She's a walking American flag. Very patriotic. Very Betty Slater.

"Welcome, welcome, welcome!" she says. "Were you all at the 4th of July parade today? Dale and I thought we might see you."

As usual, Mrs. Graham answers for her whole family. "We were only there until they announced the winners of the boat float competition! It was Mae and Cubby, which was a wonderful surprise! Although, I suppose Beau wasn't surprised, seeing as how he was a judge! Then we headed straight to Big Mama's so Santa could visit Daisy!"

Mr. Graham puffs up his chest. He's wearing a Christmas vest and turtleneck. "I did a pretty good job playing the part of Santa, if I do say so myself. Only problem is, I've still got some glue stuck to my face. Elaine used too much to paste the beard on."

"Shhh!" Mrs. Graham puts a finger up to her lips. "*You* weren't Santa, dear. *The real* Santa came."

Brady smirks. "Based on the smell of mothballs, I'd have to say *the real Santa* stores his suit in our attic."

Mrs. Graham smacks his shoulder. "Now, you just hush. You too, Phil. You're both such spoil sports." She shakes her head, and I cut my gaze to Kasey, who catches my eye and smiles. Her family is nuts, but I love them all. More than is good for me, that's for sure.

"Darby and Olivia and Tess were great sports," Mrs. Graham continues. "They found elf costumes at the church garage sale for only fifty cents each, and convinced Daisy to sit on *Santa's* lap so he could ask her what she wants for Christmas. That sweet little thing wouldn't answer, of course. So Mac went ahead and told everyone Daisy'd been a good girl all year even though some of us wonder if that's true. Then we got some pictures of Daisy with Santa before she started to cry and—"

"Take a breath, Elaine," Mr. Graham interrupts. Then he chuckles. "You must be dangerously low on oxygen by now."

While Mrs. Graham glares at him, my mom pipes up. "Why don't we all head into the backyard for some snacks before the show?"

She guides Mr. and Mrs. Graham out onto the deck, while I try to catch Kasey's eye again. But she's got her focus on the stairs. Natalie's at the top, waltzing down. As soon as my sister reaches the ground floor, Kasey sidles over to me. "Hey there, Beau," she coos. "You're looking handsome tonight."

Ah. Now I get it. Kasey was stalling until Natalie showed up so she and Brady could both witness our performance. "You too, Kasey," I choke. "I mean, you don't look handsome. You look ... beautiful."

"Thank you, kind sir." She takes my hand, lifts it overhead, and spins herself around. She's ridiculous. And adorable. I just want to spin her for the rest of my life.

Brady cocks his head. "You feeling all right there, Kase?"

Kasey blinks at him. Eyes big like Bambi. The innocent kind, not the deer-in-headlights kind. "Whatever do you mean, brother dear?"

"She's fine," I jump in to answer. "We're fine. Everything's fine." My throat is tight and hot, and I'm totally rethinking this charade. Yes, I promised Kasey. But if Brady's not all right with

Fake Us, he'll never be all right with Real Us. And what if I want Kasey for real?

I want Kasey for real.

Natalie wrinkles her nose. "Why is everyone talking weird? And acting weird. You're all so weird!"

Kasey flashes her a smile that's big and white. "Maybe we ate some of your special brownies."

Natalie turns to me. "I have no idea what Kasey's talking about," she says, "but you look like you've been caught with your hands in the cookie jar. Stop being a cookie-jar thief, Beau."

I open my mouth to protest, but I'm saved by my dad, who appears at the door leading to the deck. "Kids! You should get out here. The fireworks will be starting soon, and you don't want to miss 'em. Come on now. All four of you."

We head outside where my parents and Mr. and Mrs. Graham are already waiting for us. Boats are floating, their lights twinkling on the water. The lake reflects a crescent moon and a row of trees along the shore.

"Grab yourselves a drink and a popper or a sparkler if you want," my dad says. "I've got folding chairs set up over there." He points across the deck. "Or you can stand." He shrugs. "Either way, once the fireworks start, the best view will be over at the railing."

"Let's go," Kasey says, leading me toward the darkest corner. Her small hand heats up my whole body. Every part of me she touches feels branded. I want to tell her I'm all hers, but this isn't the right time. Natalie and Brady are across the deck from us, talking and laughing with our parents.

Kasey squeezes my hand, and the fireworks start with a series of pops. Bright webs of color light the sky, dripping downward before disappearing. More fireworks explode. Pop! Pop! Pop! Everyone oohs and ahhs with each brilliant burst.

"Isn't this lovely," my mother exclaims. I look down at Kasey and think, *Absolutely.*

She gazes up at me, and her bright eyes burrow straight into my heart. "Are you ready?" she asks. When I nod, she whispers, "Me too." Then she goes up on her toes and brushes her mouth against mine. My lips. Her lips. Soft as I remember. Riper than cherries. All I want to do is gather her in my arms, but I hold back. Let her take the lead. Kasey tips her chin, leaning into me, and I lose myself in the sweetness of her.

She tastes like magic. Like sunshine. Like every delicious thing I can imagine. My hands find her waist, pulling her close. It's not a grip—she's still free—but she relaxes into my embrace. Her kiss is a sigh of surrender. When we pause for breath, she lowers herself off her toes and presses her cheek to my chest. I'm sure she can feel my heart banging against my ribs. But I don't care. I'm done pretending.

"Kasey," I murmur. She's so warm and light in my arms. "You have no idea how long I've dreamed of kissing you like this. It feels like I've been waiting my whole life."

"Beau!" Brady calls out, startling Kasey and me apart. He and Natalie are heading our way, eyes on us, ignoring the fireworks. He probably wants to rip me apart, and my pulse races, but I have no regrets. Kasey's worth any fight. All for her. For always.

"Listen, Brady," I begin. My voice sounds dredged up from the lake.

"What's happening here, man?"

"I'm glad you asked that," Kasey answers before I can. "It's time you and Natalie knew the truth. Beau and I. *We're* what's happening."

"You and Beau?" Natalie grips the railing, and Brady squints. Like squeezing his eyes shut might make this go away.

Kasey slides back into my arms. "Don't tell me you haven't noticed."

Another set of fireworks pops above us, and Kasey prods my side. I don't know what she wants me to say, but it doesn't much matter because my mouth is frozen. Turns out I've got no acting skills, and I honestly care about Kasey too much to fake my feelings. After a beat, she shifts her focus to my sister. "What about you, Nat? You didn't catch on to the fact that your brother and I are crazy about each other?"

"Say it, Beau," Brady growls. "I need to hear this from you."

My throat is sandpaper, but I grit out the words. "I'm crazy about your sister."

Natalie peers at Kasey. "You and Beau?" she repeats. "For real?"

Kasey lifts her chin. "I hope that doesn't bother you." She turns to Brady. "Or you either. But even if you're both bothered—even if you absolutely hate the thought of us together—you'll have to get used to it. Because"—she shifts in my arms, gazing up at me—"we are head over heels in love."

Natalie shrieks.

"What's going on over there?" my dad calls out. All four parents look our way as a string of fireworks illuminates the deck. It's like the sun is shining on Kasey. In my arms. Their jaws all drop.

"Kasey?" squawks Mrs. Graham.

"Beau?" My mother gasps.

I wrap my arms tighter around Kasey. At least I'm not lying to anyone. "It's true," I say. "I'm totally in love with Kasey."

"Well." Nat waves her sparkler and grins. "It's about time."

Chapter Thirteen

KASEY

Natalie turns to Brady, fluffs her blonde curls, and makes a kissy-face noise. "Did you hear that? My brother and your sister are *totally in looooove!*"

"That seems to be the case," Brady says. "So. Mission accomplished?"

They both high-five each other, then they switch to downlowing, as if that's even a thing. Next they do a weird hip-bump dance, frolicking around the deck like they just won the lottery.

Meanwhile, my arms break out in goosebumps, and I spin around to face Beau. "Did you know about this?" A flush creeps up my throat, spreading to my cheeks, and *oh no, no, no, no, no.* "Please tell me you didn't set me up again. If this is another one of your pranks ..."

Beau's face goes as white as my blouse. Either that, or the lights from the fireworks make him look like he's seen a ghost. Or he *is* a ghost. Wait. Is that it? Are we dead?

Pretty much nothing else makes sense right now. And our parents seem just as baffled. They've moved into a semicircle formation, staring at us, sparklers hanging at their sides.

"Kasey Elizabeth!" My mom's the first to start talking.

Shocker. "I thought you and Beau didn't like each other. Isn't that what you told me?"

"Yes!" Mrs. Slater pipes up. "That's what I thought too." Her gaze shifts between me and Beau and Nat and Brady. "Have you kids all been drinking? Or ..." She whispers, "Are you doing the drugs?"

This finally gets Natalie to stop dancing. At least her body stops. Her eyes are still totally dancing. Then she chuckles. "I can assure you *the drugs* aren't the case here, Mother. Right, Brady?"

"Affirmative." Brady salutes the group.

My mom turns to Brady. "Then what *is* the case?"

"Sorry, man." Brady claps Beau on the back. "But Nat and I figured out a long time ago that you and Kasey were into each other."

Natalie leans over to chime in. "This is true."

"We also knew you'd never get together if we suggested it directly."

Nat nods. "Also true."

Brady slings an arm around Beau's sister. "The real trick for Nat and me was hitting just the right level of sibling disinterest. We wanted your relationship to feel irresistible. But not *impossible*."

"Well, the joke's on you," I choke out, and the group shifts their focus back to me. "Because Beau and I feel nothing for each other. We aren't in love. We never have been. We were just fooling all of *you* tonight."

"Yeah, I don't think so," Natalie says.

Pop, pop, pop!

Another round of fireworks explodes at the same time my heart is imploding. But I ignore my traitorous insides and turn to my mom. "Come on, Mom. Admit it. You and Mrs. Slater have been master strategists, arranging for Beau and me to be together for days."

My mom and Mrs. Slater exchange shrugs, and I glance at Beau, who's fixated on his feet. Do I really have to Scooby Doo this thing for everyone by myself? And why do I feel like throwing up?

Overhead, the fireworks finale lights up the sky. Brady and Nat look at each other. My mom and dad look at each other. Mr. and Mrs. Slater look at each other. Then, as if they all heard the punchline at the same time, they all start cracking up.

Whoa. I take a step backward, knocked off balance. This is not the reaction I expected. Beau finally cuts his gaze my way, and his eyes are so warm and kind. *He's* so warm and kind. And generous. Not to mention gallant. It's an old-fashioned word for a modern guy. But I can't think about any of that right now. Not when everybody's laughing at me.

"What's so funny?" I ask, heat clawing up my throat.

My mom covers her mouth, stifling a giggle. "Kasey. Dear. I don't know what conspiracy theorist got ahold of you, but Betty and I were just trying to have a nice holiday with all our kids home at the same time. If you and Beau thought we had some other agenda, one involving you two ...well ..." Her voice trails off for possibly the first time in my life.

Mrs. Slater nods. "I'm sorry if you felt manipulated, but I promise we weren't scheming behind your backs." She reaches out to touch Beau's shoulder with one hand, and mine with the other. She's awfully gentle for a master strategist. Which means she's probably not one.

I turn to Brady. "If you really wanted Beau and me together, why were you always such a jerk every time I was near you two?"

"You mean back when I was fifteen?" He cracks a smile. "Newsflash, Kase. Not wanting your little sister hanging around is pretty normal behavior for a big brother."

Ugh. Brady isn't wrong. Which means I probably am.

A chill runs up my spine, and I glance at Natalie. "What about you, Nat? The Ex-Lax brownies? You *definitely* hated me."

She snorts. "I was just jealous. I had a huge crush on Grantly Bender, but he was totally and hopelessly infatuated with you."

"He was?" Gulp. "I had no idea."

"Apparently, you miss some clues sometimes," she says, darting her eyes at Beau. "But for the record, I'd never *actually* slip something in someone else's food. Plus that was years ago, and I'm pretty awesome now." She fluffs her hair again. "So can we all agree to let Beforeland go?"

"Of course." I swallow hard, trying not to feel ridiculous. I should be *happy* that nobody actually had it out for me. That I'm the only one who's been stuck in *Beforeland*. But tonight was supposed to be my turn to turn the tables. To make someone else feel dumb for once. Now here I am feeling ... dumb. Again.

Poisoned by the taste of your own medicine.

Brady chuckles. "I won't lie. I was pretty jealous too."

I press a palm to my flaming cheek. "Of what?"

"I wasn't crushing on Grantly Bender or anything," he says, "but I didn't want to lose my best friend to my sister. Or lose you to Beau." He bumps my shoulder. "You were my little buddy, Kase. And you were also *really* fun to torment." He tilts his head at Beau. "So I recruited *this guy* to mess with you, hoping you'd keep away from him." Brady's mouth goes crooked. "Then we grew up. And it took me about three seconds to figure out you and Beau have real feelings for each other."

Beau shifts his jaw and his weight, but he says nothing.

"Yep," Natalie chimes in. "Beau would always ask about you without *asking* about you, you know?"

"And *you* only came home when Beau wasn't going to be here," Brady adds. "So when I found out you'd both be here for the 4th—" he tilts his head at Natalie—"I recruited *this girl* to help me get you and Beau together."

"That's why we didn't judge the floats," Nat says.

"And why we left you to ride in the back of Uncle Cubby's truck," Brady adds.

Natalie curtsies to Brady. "We made a great team."

"Indeed." Brady bows.

"Man." Beau blows out a long breath, long enough that it's

clear he wasn't in on any of this. "You could've just told me," he says.

"What?" Brady splays his hands. "And ruin this good time?"

While they've all been talking, the earth has been slowly slipping out from under me. Everything I believed is flipped on its axis now, and I can't tell who or what I can trust. Especially my heart. I open my mouth, completely unsure about the words that might come out, but my mother beats me to it.

"Speaking of good times," she exclaims, "How about those snickerdoodles? Should we get the dessert portion of the evening started?"

"Yes!" Mrs. Slater claps her hands. "I'll break out the ice cream!" My father and Mr. Slater don't have to be told twice. They make a beeline for the cookies. Natalie and Brady cast glances at each other, then follow them inside. I just stand there frozen. Every move I made tonight was wrong. So where do I go from here?

"Kasey."

I turn to face Beau, and my stomach is in knots. I dragged a good man into a bad plan. And my knee-jerk reaction would be to blame my brother. But like Natalie said, that was Beforeland. Afterland is on me. "I'm so sorry I got you mixed up in this," I say softly. "But don't worry. I'm the one who looks like the idiot. Not you. Not at all." I force a small smile. "Your golden reputation remains intact."

"I don't care about my reputation." He reaches out to gather my hands in his, and my skin zings at his touch. I'd better get that under control. But control is hard when he smells so good and his mouth's so soft and—*Stop it, Kasey.*

In two days, I'm flying back to California, and Beau's flying off to who knows where. Someplace important. Causes that need him. All those charities he donates his proceeds to ... I can't put a damper on his philanthropic spirit. Beau told me himself he loves his job. And mine is thousands of miles from his. I've kept myself distant for so long. I can keep going if it's the right thing to do. Beau deserves better than to be tethered to me.

"Anyway, I'm sorry." I swallow hard. "About all of it."

"Well, I'm not." Beau meets my gaze and holds it steady, speaking with his eyes. Speaking to my soul. "Kasey." He draws in a long breath, then exhales. "I have feelings for you." His voice is hoarse, like he's been shouting the same words forever, but I never heard him in Beforeland. "I have *all* the feelings for you," he says. "Every single one of them. I always have." When he squeezes my hands, all the air leaves my lungs.

"Oh," I whisper, but it's barely a sound because right now I'm barely breathing. My brain's running a slideshow of all the times I buried my own feelings. I drew horns in Sharpie on pictures of Beau when I wanted to write *KEG* on his heart.

"I've also got something to show you." He releases one of my hands to dig in his back pocket. "This is what I was planning to give you, that day after graduation." From behind his back he produces a bracelet, a rope of braided gold, cupped in his palm. It sparkles in a sliver of moonlight and the countless stars above us.

"It's beautiful." I gulp, and he looks down as if he's seeing the thing in his hand for the first time himself.

"I knew you couldn't wait to get out into the world," he says. "That once you got a taste of life outside of Abieville, you might be gone for good. Especially after the way Brady and I treated you. So I decided to give you this charm bracelet and ask you to meet me back here every summer. I figured I'd offer you a new charm each year. It was an excuse to keep you coming home. One way I could keep seeing you." He ducks his head, and my insides ache at the thoughtfulness of his plan. This isn't some throwaway token from a teenage guy who felt guilty. This gift has soul in it. Beau's soul.

"There's only one charm so far," he says.

I peer down into his hand, and the charm slowly takes shape in the darkness. "Is that ... a ... cat?" I giggle, from nerves or joy or maybe fear. "That's ... kind of ... random."

Beau chuckles. "Yeah, I didn't have much game with girls back then. And I wasn't sure how you'd take the whole charm bracelet idea in the first place. So I thought I'd start out small. And I knew you loved Sprinkles, so."

I lift my head and smile. "I take it back. This is not random at all. A cat charm is perfect."

His smile is bashful in the best kind of way. "I was hoping if things went well, I'd get to add a new charm every year. So Sprinkles wouldn't be lonely. But ..."

I scrunch up my nose. "Things didn't go well."

My insides begin to unravel, remembering all those years we spent competing. Side by side. We always were together, going after the same things. Beau made sure he was with me, but I never let myself imagine there was a reason beyond him wanting to win. I couldn't risk thinking he had deeper feelings. I was too busy guarding mine.

He moves an inch closer to me. "We were so young. Maybe things weren't meant to go well back then. What if the universe planned to give us a second chance all along?" He holds up the bracelet and it dangles in front of me, twisting and free.

I raise my wrist. "Let's see if it fits. Like Cinderella and her glass slipper. You know. If there'd been a cat hanging off her heel." Beau reaches out to wrap the chain around it. And as he clicks the clasp shut, my heart begins to swell, filling up with a thousand balloons until there's no room left for anything else. Except maybe light and happiness, because I've got all the feelings too. Just like Beau said. For so many years, I denied it, but I can't pretend anymore. My whole balloon-filled heart is beating for Beau.

"Looks like it fits," he says, lifting my hand. Then he gently brushes his lips against my wrist. The move is so tender, I almost melt immediately, right here on the Slaters' deck. When he places both palms on my cheeks—softly, and with so much care—I stand on my toes to wrap my arms around his neck. And as my fingers tangle in his hair, one of his hands slips to my chin. He tips my face up while he lowers his. Our lips are only a breath apart.

"Kasey," he whispers.

"Kasey!" My mother bursts from the Slaters' house, waving my phone in the air. "Judy Witherspoon from *The Chronicle* is calling!"

Chapter Fourteen

BEAU

Kasey's eyes go wide, and a knife slashes through my guts. "Take the call," I tell her. Without a word, she sprints to her mom to grab her phone. Above me, the air fills with the pops and whistles of a few latecomer fireworks. People all over Abieville are still celebrating independence, but I don't want to be set free. Forget the 4th of July. Forget life without Kasey.

Freedom is overrated.

I watch as Kasey makes her way over to the side of our house, the phone cupped to her ear. Right now this Judy Witherspoon person is probably offering her the job she's been hoping to get for years. Scratch that. For her whole life. My shoulders slump.

Timing is everything, Beau. And as always, your timing is garbage.

The rest of the Grahams and my family file out of the house and gather around me. We shuffle our feet, shift our weight. Yeah. The moment's pretty awkward. Everyone's already figured out how I feel about Kasey. Now we're standing around, thinking the same thing: that a future with Kasey will be impossible if she takes this job in California.

My work consists entirely of freelance gigs. How could we even build a relationship living thousands of miles apart? Not to mention, the assignments I take are unpredictable—in location and duration.

Within minutes, Kasey reappears around the corner, trudging slowly, her head hanging low. My heart leaps into my throat. Whoa. She didn't get hired? Any newspaper would be lucky to have her. Judy Witherspoon must be the world's biggest fool.

Wait. Hold up there, my friend. Who's the real fool here?

Me.

I let Kasey Graham get away first, years ago. Instead of acknowledging her beauty, intelligence, and strength, I made her doubt herself. I knew how special she was, and I watched her go. No, I practically pushed her away with both hands. Not literally. But all those years of pranking and teasing with Brady were worse than a shove. I took the things Kasey wanted most, when all I really wanted was her. Correction: *Is* her.

But I'm done making that mistake.

Kasey joins our circle, squeezing in between my mom and me. She sniffles and rubs at her nose. Oh, man. My stomach knives are back and sharper than ever. I didn't want Kasey to go, but I didn't want her hurting either. I hate seeing her sad, even if her tears mean a silver lining for me.

Correction: For *us*.

Still, I feel terrible, and I'm not alone. Everyone bends their heads at sympathetic angles. Kasey's mom speaks up first. "I'm so sorry, dear. Keep your chin up. There will be other jobs. Other newspapers."

My mother goes next, placing a hand on Kasey's shoulder. "Oh yes, sweetie. This is so true. I remember when Beau was just starting out, and he got turned down for a few shoots. My, my. He was so disappointed. It just about broke my heart, I must admit." She cranes her neck past Kasey to see me. "But just look at him now." Her tone brightens. "My award-winning son. So in demand. People clamor to book him for their projects months in advance. In fact his next assignment is with a Pulitzer-Prize winner!"

"What?" Kasey's head jerks up, and she turns to me. "You didn't tell me that."

My mom casts a shy glance my way. "Oh, you know my boy. He's always been so humble. Beau never likes to brag."

Brady smirks. "That doesn't sound like the Beau I know."

I shake my head. "Thanks, man. Love you too." I could give Brady a hard time for taking a shot at me now, but the guy's just trying to lighten the mood for his sister's sake. So I give him a pass. Then I turn to Kasey. "It's okay, Kase. I've been doing some thinking."

She sniffs again. "About what?"

"The future. Our future." I know she's crushed, so I try to sound as gentle and supportive as I can. "Why don't you tag along with me on my next assignment? I've got plenty of pull with the team, and who knows? Something could crop up for you on the road. Most of the photographers I've worked with can't write copy to save their lives. We could use someone who's good with words."

"What a wonderful idea!" Mrs. Graham says. "My Kasey is absolutely excellent with words. She always has been. Even as a little girl—just three years old—she pretended to write. She could barely hold a crayon in her little fist, but she'd tell me she was making a book. *Making a book!* It was the cutest thing." She looks at Kasey, then swipes at her own eyes. I can't tell if she's crying or laughing, but I know she's definitely still talking. "Yes, when it comes to words, my girl is the very best." She shifts her focus to the whole group. "She gets that from me, you know."

Mr. Graham takes his wife's hand. "She sure does, Elaine." He pulls her toward him and wraps an arm around her. "But let's leave Kasey to talk to Beau now. All of us. I'm guessing she's gotten enough of a pep talk from us old folks tonight."

"Good idea, Phil," my dad says. "And we can still have those cookies, right?" After some quiet grumbling and a few pats on Kasey's shoulder, everyone heads back into the house. Soon Kasey and I are alone again, standing at the railing overlooking the lake.

She looks up at me and sighs. Long and loud. From deep down inside.

"Hey." I reach for her hand. The moon lights her face. "How are you holding up?" She says nothing, just shakes her head. I give her fingers a squeeze. "I hope I didn't sound like too much of a caveman back there. *Me Man. Take care of Woman.*" I try on a chuckle, but a single tear rolls down Kasey's face. That's the exact opposite of what I wanted.

"Beau." Her voice is thick with emotion. "I don't need a pity job."

"Believe me, I know that. And I don't go in for that macho stuff either, so I'm sorry if that's the impression I gave. But I'm not sorry about wanting to take care of you, Kasey."

She drops her chin. "I don't need you to take care of me either."

I blow out a breath. This is coming out all wrong, and I'm just upsetting the woman I love, when all I want to do is make life easier for her. To make a life *with* her. "What if we—"

"Stop. Please." She looks up and swallows so hard I can practically hear it. Another late, lone firecracker pops somewhere in the distance. "Just listen to me, okay?"

"Okay." I reach out to stroke her bare arm. It's soft. Smooth. Perfect. The July air is warm and sweet. I want to take Kasey in my arms and soak her up. Claim her as mine. But Kasey's got to get her sadness off her chest first. "I'm listening."

She chews at her lip. "I don't need your pity, and I don't need you to take care of me, because I can take care of myself."

"Of course you can. You're the strongest, smartest person I know. And I—"

"I got the job, Beau."

My throat constricts. "You what?"

"At *The Chronicle*. Judy Witherspoon just offered me the position. Well, first she apologized for interrupting the fireworks. She forgot I was on the east coast, and wanted to share the good news as soon as possible. And then she hired me."

My lungs are exploding, and I start to stammer. "Oh. I. Wow. You ... I didn't ... Congratulations."

"Thanks." She gives me a tight nod. "Anyway, this job couldn't have come at a better time." *Great.* I feel sick. Kasey's leaving me, and she thinks it's a good thing? "I had an hourly contract there all through college, but I can't afford LA rent without a full-time salary."

"Right." My jaw goes rigid. Bear-trap tight. "Good. Yeah. Got it."

Her eyes widen, and she starts talking faster, like she's trying to convince me how great this is. Maybe she's trying to convince herself. "They made me head of Classifieds, Beau. I know it doesn't sound like much, but it's a really big deal. I'll be the youngest department head at the paper."

"That's ... amazing." I unclench my teeth and force my mouth into a smile. I want to support her on the outside even though inside I'm dying. "So I guess those were happy tears then."

"Huh?" She cocks her head. Blinks a few times.

"When you first walked over after the call. The sniffles. You wiped your nose. I thought you were crying." I level my gaze and watch as Kasey's eyes get wet. She rubs at them with her fists. "Hey. You *are* crying."

"Maybe a little." She sniffs and nods again. "But I wouldn't say happy tears. Not exactly. I think ..." Her voice catches. "The feeling is closer to pride." She shakes her head. "I've spent my entire life trying to get people's approval. To be worthy. To finally believe I'm good enough." She blows out a long breath. "I'm not even sure how to handle these emotions. It's all kind of overwhelming." I put my hands on her shoulders, and she shivers even though the night's still warm.

"For the record, I always believed in you, Kase. And I'll always be your biggest fan."

She looks down and starts fumbling at her wrist, working the clasp of her bracelet with one hand.

What is happening?

"Your bracelet. It's so beautiful. And the charm idea ..." Her breath hitches, and she gulps. "It's so sweet. It's so *you*." Lifting her face again, Kasey peers up at me from under wet lashes. "But there's a whole life out there waiting for you. A big, important life. People are counting on you to document their stories. To contribute to their causes." She takes a beat. "Not to mention your own vision." Her eyes are shining in the moonlight, and my heart is pumping hard. "A Pulitzer-Prize winner wants to work with you, Beau. That's ... it's ... beyond incredible. It's what you've always wanted, and I don't want to hold you back from that. I won't keep you chained down, waiting around to give me charms. Not when you could be out there really living."

My heart pumps even faster. "But I don't feel chained."

"You wouldn't be completely free, though." She inhales deeply, breathes out. "Not if you're always thinking about me."

"Kasey. Please." I hate sounding desperate, but I am. "I don't care about any of that."

"Okay." She nods. "Then I'll care *for* you." Her voice is soft now, like she's already a country away. She rubs at her bare wrist. "Your real dream isn't here." She looks out over the lake. "It's out there. Thousands of miles from this place."

I make a sound in the back of my throat—part wounded animal, part broken man. If she'd taken an axe and chopped me down the middle, I couldn't feel more cut in two. "Kasey. Don't you get it? You're my dream. You."

She tucks the bracelet into my hand. "For your sake, I can't let that be true."

Chapter Fifteen

KASEY

For my family's fake Christmas Eve, my nose is right on theme, turning as red as good old Rudolph's—with both a PH and an F. I haven't stopped crying. I didn't sleep. And I absolutely can't eat. Not my mom's Christmas Eve pancakes for breakfast. Or her Christmas Eve BLTs for lunch. And I really, really love bacon.

But giving that bracelet back to Beau shattered my heart into ten million pieces. One for every minute I'll spend away from him for the rest of my life.

Still, saying goodbye to him was the right thing to do. If not for me, then definitely for him. He doesn't need me weighing down his future, and I don't want him worrying about mine. It's way past time I start believing in myself and reaching for my own potential. And I'm totally going to do the whole reach-for-my potential thing. Right after I dry my tears (again) and try to act thrilled about our pretend Christmas Eve.

As per my mother's detailed instructions, we're all supposed to forget it's three in the afternoon. On the 5th of July. During a heat wave. Today is basically the opposite of a winter wonderland. I might've skipped all the proceedings, except Big Mama is finally feeling better. So the whole family is rallying and festive. Including me.

I've just gotten dressed in a bright-red wrap dress (hopefully distracting from my nose) when Brady knocks on my door and pokes his head in. I wave him inside. "Hey, sis." His voice is uncharacteristically quiet. I take one look at his face, those brows knitted together, and fresh tears spring into my eyes.

"Merry Christmas Eve," I choke out.

"You too," he says. "But you're gonna need to practice sounding merrier before you leave this room."

I gulp and shift my weight. "Thanks for the tip."

Brady's mouth slips into a grim line. "So I think you should know, Beau stopped by my place about an hour ago. The poor guy looked even more wrecked than you do. I mean—not to say you look bad. You look great. Really ... pretty."

This makes me snort. A snotty snort. "You're a terrible liar."

"Anyway." He rakes a hand across his forehead. "I'm really sorry, Kase. About last night. About everything."

I grab a tissue to wipe my nose for the ten-millionth time. "Not your fault," I sniffle.

"Well." He clears his throat. "What happened after graduation was. *Is*. And I never apologized to you." The crackle in his voice suggests he's being sincere. "Saying I'm sorry to you would've meant admitting I did something wrong in the first place. And since you never ratted Beau and me out ... well. I thought we got away with it." He bobs his head. "So. This is me. Officially apologizing to you, Kase. Especially if any of that mess back then ruined things for you and Beau now."

I toss the tissue on my dresser and throw myself at my brother. He hugs me back awkwardly—the kind where he's mostly frozen, just patting my back.

"Thank you, Brady." I sniffle into his shoulder.

"Hey. I'm not a Kleenex," he mumbles. This makes me laugh for the first time in a while. And when I pull away, his eyes are misty. We both take a beat, then we make faces at each other—sticking our tongues out to switch back to our old familiar routines. "You all right?" he asks.

"Maybe." I nod. Swallow. Nod. "Or at least I will be. I think. Either way, as of today, I'm owning my choices. The good and the bad. They're on me now. Not on you. And certainly not on the you from when we were kids. Deal?"

His smile is shy, but he meets my gaze. "Deal. But for the record, I still think you and Beau could be great together."

"Please, Brady." My eyes are stinging again. "If you really want to help me, you won't bring him up again."

"Today?"

I sigh. "Ever. Not even to update me when he wins his own Pulitzer, okay?" My shoulders sink. "I'll just assume Beauregard Slater ends up famous and happily married to somebody perfect. And that ending things with him was worth the sacrifice."

"Fine." Brady wrinkles his nose. "I promise never to talk about Beau again. After this one last time." He steps out into the hall and returns with a large box. It's covered in green paper and tied with red raffia. There's a sprig of holly in the knot. The package is beautiful. "Beau asked me to give this to you."

Despite the ache in my stomach, my lips curve up. Almost a smile. "That does not look like a Beau Slater wrap job."

Brady chuckles. "It's possible Natalie wrapped this for him. But the gift is definitely from Beau. He said you'd know what it meant."

I groan. "You keep saying his name."

"Are you going to open it, or not?"

"Not."

The angle of my brother's brow says he's about to switch into debate mode, but my mother calls to us from the living room, interrupting. "Kids! Big Mama's here. Come on down!"

I flash back to all the Christmas Eves from my childhood when my aunts and uncles would send the cousins down to our grandparents' basement. While the grownups displayed the presents and got the living room holiday-ready, the ten kids would hunker down, waiting to be called upstairs together. Even though we knew what was coming—our yearly ornaments and matching Christmas pajamas—we still had so much fun.

Some of my favorite memories are of splitting into teams to play while our parents set up. Boys against girls. Elders against Littlers. Sometimes we'd break into four teams, one for each family. We'd play Charades or Twenty Questions. Truth or Dare. Dark Tag. Nobody much cared about winning, which was good because just when we'd be reaching the end of the game, Big Mama would come down to collect us.

Today she's still recovering from her stomach bug, so instead of coming to us, she's settled on the couch. Actually, it's more like the couch is swallowing her. At most, Big Mama is five feet tall and ninety pounds soaking wet. But she's definitely gotten into the Christmas-in-July spirit. She's paired green corduroy slacks with a red turtleneck, and she's got an angel halo stuck in her creampuff hair.

"Kasey!" Her blue eyes widen, and she reaches for my hand. After I kiss her papery cheek, she checks me out from head to toe. "You look simply wonderful." Her voice is wobbly, but her gaze is clear. "I am so very happy to see you."

My heart almost bursts. "I am so very happy to see you too."

"Ahem." Brady leans in. "What am I, Big Mama? Chopped liver?"

"Oh, Brady." She waves his comment away. "Your sister hasn't been home in ages, and I see plenty of you." She tilts her head, and her halo slips. "Besides. Chopped liver is delicious. That's hardly an insult."

Brady chuckles. "I'll take your word for it."

"Good boy," she says. "Now go help your mother in the kitchen, so I can catch up with my granddaughter." She pats the cushion beside her. "Come. Sit, Kasey. Let's have a chat."

I take a seat and help her readjust her halo. "How are you doing, Big Mama?"

"Oh, you know." She sighs. "Taking it one meal at a time."

Her head bobbles like it's too heavy for her neck. "I kept my Christmas Eve pancakes down, so that's progress."

I lay a hand on her knee and squeeze. "That's excellent news." I was actually wondering how she's been holding up without Big Papa. But if she wants to talk about breakfast instead of her feelings, I completely understand. They were together for most of her life. That's a loss I can't even imagine.

"How about you, dear?" She pats my hand. "A little birdy told me there might be a new man in your life." She peeks around the room and lowers her voice. "That little birdy is your mother."

Shocker.

"Nope." My insides churn. But for Big Mama's sake, I'll force a smile, even if it makes my face crack off. "No man for me." Churn. Smile. Crack. "But I did get a new job I'm pretty excited about. More like a promotion. At the newspaper."

"*The Chronicle.*" She beams.

"Exactly." My smile suddenly feels less forced. "I started there years ago as an unpaid intern. Now I'm a department head."

"Well, isn't that wonderful. Rewarding work is so important for a smart young woman like you. Whether that work is in the home or somewhere else." She stares off into the distance like she's calling up the past. "I was a librarian at the Abieville Library for years. Did you know that, dear?"

"I did know, yes." My smile is genuine now. "I always thought that was pretty great."

"Well, I caused quite the stir back then." She clucks. *Ahhhh. That's where my mom gets it.* "Keeping my job after Remy was born wasn't the norm in Abieville," she says. "But I loved the library, and I loved my daughter, and I didn't want to leave either of them. So I just brought the baby to work with me." She raises a wispy eyebrow, remembering. "Eventually everyone got used to her. Remy was our little library mascot."

And now I'm grinning. "I don't think I'll be bringing any babies to *The Chronicle*. It's not exactly a family friendly office."

"Then that's probably wise." She shifts her focus back to me.

"The important thing to remember is you've got choices, Kasey. You can do anything. Be anything. Have anything. Your heart just has to want it badly enough." She reaches out to clasp my hand. "The world is your oyster, dear. Just be sure to choose the *right* oyster."

My stomach clenches at the metaphor. Big Mama couldn't possibly know how hard my choices have been this week. Or could she? Either way, she seems a whole lot sharper than Mom led me to believe. I take a deep breath and let it leak out slowly.

"What is it, dear?" she asks.

"I don't know." I shake my head. "I guess I wish choosing could be easier."

"Ah. Well." She shrugs. "Whenever I can't decide, I just order one of each oyster on the menu." Her eyes begin to sparkle. "Sometimes I end up eating a dozen by myself, but at least I never have regrets."

"Hold on. Is this still an oyster metaphor? Or are you talking about oysters for real now?"

"Maybe both." She blinks at me. "I'm just glad you're home for Christmas."

Over the next half hour, the rest of Big Mama's family trickles in. Aunts. Uncles. Cousins. Even Ford, who worked the overnight shift, so when he falls asleep in a corner chair, nobody tries to wake him. Letty and Three and Nella take turns handing out Big Mama's gifts. Everyone knows what's in the boxes, but we all act surprised anyway.

According to tradition, we open gifts in order from youngest to oldest, which means Daisy—the only great grandchild at this point—goes first. We all ignore her no-talking thing, engaging in one-sided questions and answers. I love that about us. Weird is normal for my family. Plus my mom talks enough for all of us.

After we've hung our new ornaments on the cousins' tree, Mom splits us up into different rooms to change into our new pajamas. They're all Buddy-the-Elf themed, with bright green tops and yellow bottoms. Quotes from the movie are printed

THAT TIME I KISSED MY BROTHER'S BEST FRIEND

across the backside. We do our usual fashion show, walking the "runway" in front of the tree, reading the quotes out loud.

Tess got: *Smiling's my favorite!*

Darby has: *What's your favorite color?*

Liv's says: *That's not very shiny.*

When Brady takes his turn, I bust out laughing. "*You smell like beef and cheese*? Brady! That's hilarious!"

He wags a finger at Big Mama. "Did you give these to me on purpose?"

"Well." I smirk. "If the stink fits..."

"Ha ha." He smirks back. "Laugh it up, Fuzzball." It's an inside joke we've shared since the first time we watched the original *Star Wars* together. Of course this is *my* cue to start acting like a Chewbacca. And if I do say so myself, I have pretty-much perfected my Wookie.

My first growl makes Brady chuckle, so I growl again. This time louder. By now my cousins are all cracking up. Even my aunts and uncles join in the laughter. I'm not used to such a big spotlight, so I decide to gift everyone with one last epic howl. So I take a deep breath and really let my inner-Wookie rip. "Yaaaaarrrrggggh!" And that's when Brady shifts his focus to something beyond my shoulder. I spin around and see the open front door.

Beau.

My heart hits the floor, and I basically die of embarrassment. He ducks his head and waves. "Sorry to interrupt," he says. While my neck and throat and both my cheeks are bursting into flames, he makes his way over to me. "Guess you didn't hear me knock, huh?"

"I was being a Wookie."

"I heard. Very impressive." His lips twitch. "Nice pajamas, Chewie."

"Wowsa!" Big Mama looks Beau over from head to toe. "That's a tall oyster you've got there, Kasey."

Beau glances at her, then back at me. "Hey. Can I talk to you? Privately?"

I stand there gaping, unable to speak. Thankfully my mother rescues me. "Come on, everyone. Let's head out back to take some holiday pictures. You all look so cute in your pajamas. We'll do shots with each family individually, then a group picture at the end." She turns to me. "It might take me a while to get this all arranged, Kasey, so you two take your time ..."

Beau nods at her. "Thanks, Mrs. Graham."

"Call me Elaine," she says. Then she claps her hands to rally the troops. "Okay! Let's go people!" Uncle Irv and Auntie Ann move first, helping Big Mama out to the backyard. Everyone else follows suit, casting quick peeks at Beau before heading out the glass slider. When I hazard my own glance up at him, he's gazing down at me.

Churn. Smile. Gulp.

"I tried to be patient." He tilts his head. "But I couldn't wait anymore."

"Hold on!" Brady calls out, rushing down the stairs. I didn't see him sneak up to my room, but now he's carrying Beau's gift. He shoves the package into my arms and turns to Beau. "I tried to get her to open it earlier, man. But she wouldn't listen to me."

"That sounds like your sister," Beau says. "I love that about her."

My pulse begins to race. He *loves* that about me?

"Yeah." Brady shrugs. "Kasey's pretty stubborn, but she can be lovable too. Once you figure that out, things get easier. But the Wookie smell? *That* takes some getting used to."

"Hey!" I put my hands on my hips in mock anger, which is hard to pull off in Buddy the Elf pajamas. "Would you two stop talking about me like I can't hear you?"

Brady salutes me. "As you wish." He turns to Beau. "If you need me, I'll be outside. Taking pictures. In my beef and cheese pajamas."

Beau chuckles. "Good luck, my man."

"Same to you, friend. Same to you."

As Brady strolls outside to join the rest of my family, I can hear the sounds of their laughter. And my mother barking orders. That is until Brady shuts the back slider. Then Beau and I are truly alone. In the silence. Oh, wow.

I swallow hard. "Beau ... I—"

"First things first," he says. "Did your grandmother call me an oyster?"

This question catches me off guard, and I actually let out a snort. As if wearing Elf pajamas and howling like a Wookie wasn't embarrassing enough. "Sometimes Big Mama says things that don't totally make sense. And sometimes she knows *exactly* what she's saying."

Beau lifts an eyebrow. "I'll take your word for it." He nods at the package in my arms. "Now, will you please do me a favor and open that?"

I shift my weight. Bite my lip. Beau keeps his gaze laser-focused on me. We're both quiet for a stretch, and I'm actually holding my breath. "Please, Kasey," he says. "Then, if you still want me to leave, I'll go. As hard as leaving will be, I promise I will. If you ask me to."

I exhale. Finally. "Okay." I move to the couch and sit with Beau's gift in my lap. For such a large package, it's awfully light. I tug off the raffia and peel back the paper. Inside the large cardboard box is a smaller box. Also wrapped. "Ah." I curve my lip up on one side. "So this is how it's gonna be?"

His mouth quirks. "Maybe. Maybe not."

I unwrap two more boxes of decreasing size, and the smaller the boxes get, the more my heart aches. At the end of all this, I'll still have to ask Beau to walk away. I only want what's best for him. And I'm not best. "I might as well tell you if you're giving me the bracelet back ... I can't take it."

"Hmm." Beau rubs his chin. "I guess we'll see, won't we?" I lift the lid off the next box and peer inside. The box in there is tiny. "That's the last one," he says.

"Beau." My breath catches in my throat. "This can't be a ring, right? Because ... that's just crazy."

"When it comes to you, I'm all in for crazy." His voice is low and deep. "But I'd never propose without speaking to your parents first. Or without being *reasonably* sure what your answer would be. We've got a lot of conversations ahead of us between now and then." I look into his eyes. His expression is so calm. So confident. It's getting harder for me to keep any air in my lungs.

"Go on," he says.

So I suck in a breath and open the box. Sure enough, under a layer of tissue, is the charm bracelet. "Beau." My heart splits down the middle, knowing what I have to do. "I—"

"Before you try giving this back to me, just look at it." I search his face, and he smiles. "Please, Kase."

My hands tremble as I pull out the bracelet and hold it up to the light. Since last night, he's added five more charms to the chain. Along with the cat, there's now a heart and a star. A feather. A little cottage. And what looks to be a camera. Before I can even ask what this means, Beau explains.

"That cat is still Sprinkles, of course. And there's a camera for my job. And a quill for yours."

"A quill." My heart skips a beat. "Right. I get it."

"The star means a couple things." He takes the bracelet and lifts it up for me. "You're going to be a star at *The Chronicle*, Kasey. And wherever else your career takes you. I've never believed anything more, and I'm proud to be your first, biggest fan." He takes a beat. "I also want to be your last fan."

I meet his gaze, and the warmth there makes my eyes sting. "Beau."

"We're not done." He shifts the bracelet so the next charm dangles between us. "The heart? Well, I picked this because I love you, Kasey Elizabeth Graham. Always have. Always will. So a heart charm is pretty obvious. Sorry I couldn't be more symbolic." A small laugh escapes me, and tears gather in my eyes.

"Don't cry yet," he says. "We've got one more charm to go." I blink hard and fast, but a tear spills down my cheek. Beau catches it with his thumb, then takes my hand in his free one.

"The last charm is a house, because wherever your future is, that's my future too." He pauses and his Adam's apple bobs. "Whenever we're apart, I'll carry you in my heart until we're together again. Just say the word, and I will always come home to you." He leans in close. "You're my home, Kasey."

My whole body floods with love for this good, kind man, and all I can manage to blurt out is, "Yes."

Beau's eyes go wide. "Yes?"

"Wait here." I run up to my bedroom and race back down again. Breathless and giddy, I pop open my Sharpie and write on Beau's hand.

Property of KEG! Do Not Touch!

Then I let out a great big Wookie growl and start laughing and crying at the same time, while Beau wraps the bracelet around my wrist. Once it's clasped, he opens his arms and gathers me in, covering my wet face with his sweet kisses.

From behind us comes the sound of muted cheers from my entire family. They're all gathered at the sliding door, faces pressed against the glass, applauding and jumping up and down in their Christmas pajamas.

I wave at them, then plant a kiss on Beau's nose. "Not exactly the romance you expected, huh?"

He grins. "Are you kidding? We're in Abieville. This is exactly the kind of romance I expect."

"Kasey!" Big Mama pushes her way to the front of the pack and opens the slider. "Looks like you chose the right oyster!"

My dad takes her arm and helps her inside, then everyone else piles in after her. And once again our house is full of family. And so much joy. Plus all the love.

Beau leans in and whispers. "This has been the best 4th of July ever."

"It will be." I take his hand. "Once you kiss me under the mistletoe."

Chapter Sixteen

SIX MONTHS LATER — ON ACTUAL CHRISTMAS EVE

BEAU

Me: Hey, Chewbacca. I figured you'd be going to sleep soon, and I didn't want to wake you if you already were. That's why I'm texting instead of calling. Also I've got bad news, which I hate to say out loud. I'm so sorry, but it looks like I'm going to be stuck here. All incoming flights have been canceled due to an unexpected storm. I'll FaceChat you in the morning, but I know that won't be the same as being together in Abieville. I promise to make up for it. Somehow. Someway. Love you, Chewie.

Me: PS: My mom won't be happy when she finds out either.
Kasey: I just saw your text, and I tried calling you back twice, but no dice. Time differences are weird. I left a message so you'd hear my voice, but I know wifi can be spotty in some places, and I'm not even sure where you are right now. So in case you can't check your voicemail, just know I love you back, Han Solo. Enough to survive Christmas without you. As for your mom, maybe she can drown her sorrows in Auntie Ann's fruitcake. It's dense enough to absorb a lot of tears. Call me when you get this. Or text. Or FaceChat. I miss your face.

Kasey: PS: Not to rub your absence in, but my Actual Christmas Eve (ACE) pajamas are even better than the Buddy the Elf ones from July. I'm not going to tell you how cute I look, because you'll be sad and there won't be any fruitcake left. XO

I pull my phone from the carryon, and multiple notifications for Kasey's messages ping ping ping the second I switch off airplane mode. This is par for the course whenever I fly now. It's been like this for the past six months. Kasey's working harder than ever—with lots of late nights, looming deadlines, and editorial demands. Meanwhile, I juggle shifts in shoot locations, flight delays, and urgent requests for new collaborations.

It's been a challenge, but Kasey is worth every moment of compromise. Still. Christmas is one time of year I hope never to disappoint her. So as I listen to her voicemail—twice—I can't wipe the grin off my face. Spoiler alert: I'm not stuck in bad weather. I'm in Albany. Surprising Kasey. For Actual Christmas Day.

(ACD.)

Chapter Seventeen

KASEY

My head is buried back under two pillows when my mother comes into the room. I can't see her with my cheek mashed into the mattress, but this has been my mom's Christmas morning routine since way back when Brady and I were toddlers. Now that my door is open, I can smell the cinnamon rolls straight through the down in my pillows. My mom's homemade rolls are *that* delicious. Or maybe it's because our house is *that* small. It's also possible the scent is in my head. Like muscle memory. Or I might just be hungry from missing Beau. There's a gaping hole in my heart where he should be.

There always is when he's away.

"Meeeeerrrrrrry Christmas, Kaseyyyyyy!" My mother sings this out. Loudly. I brace for her telling me she could've been the next Shania Twain if she hadn't given up a music career to raise her family. But she skips that info this time. Instead she squawks, "Brady will be here any minute!"

"Mmph."

"And Daddy's been up since the crack of dawn brining the turkey to roast. It's already ten o'clock! Time to get up and see if you and your brother got presents or coal this year!"

I pull the pillows off my head and prop myself up against the headboard. Through a cloud of static-cling hair, I peer at my phone. No new messages from Beau.

"Aren't I a little old for stockings and Santa Claus, Mom?"

"There's no such thing as too old for Santa."

I swipe loose strands of hair off my face, and spit out the ones stuck to my lips. Once most of me is visible again, my mother clucks. "Oh, my, my, my." She tilts her head. "What's wrong, sweet pea?"

At least this drags a smile out of me. "First of all, you calling me sweet pea is wrong. I feel much more at home when you're reminding me I didn't go to med school, or that I broke your heart by moving to California."

"I suppose I *do* mention those things on occasion. *Very* rarely." She pats at her Mrs. Claus hat, which looks more like a doily stretched over a lump of red hair. This morning, she's squeezed into the same dress she's worn on Actual Christmas Day for decades. It's red velvet with sprigs of holly embroidered across the bust. She's also wearing a frilly white apron and black lace-up boots.

"We have different definitions of rare," I say.

"Why so grumpy, Kasey?"

"It's Beau." I shake my head. "He's not going to be here for Christmas after all." The knot in my stomach tightens. "I knew his making it here was a long shot, but I got my hopes up anyway."

"Oh, dear." My mother smooths her apron and comes over to my bedside. Then she smooths the ladybug bedspread before sitting on the edge of the mattress. "Love does tend to do that to us, Kasey. It makes us hopeful, I mean."

Her eyes are warm. Shining almost. This is weirder than her calling me sweet pea. But my mother is right. The past six months have been the happiest of my life, but also—sometimes—the hardest. The funny thing is, each time Beau leaves, I hurt a little more, but also a little less. *Less* because he's proven time and again he'll always come back to me. *More* because I know all too well now what I'm missing when he's gone.

"Hidey ho!" My dad appears in the doorway wearing a forest green sweater. It's got a giant red-nosed reindeer face on the front, with two antlers stretching up to my father's armpits. The name RudolF is stitched below. Capital F.

"No Santa Claus suit this year?" I ask.

"Santa came in the summer, remember?" He grins at me and winks. "The old boy needs his rest." He glances at my mom, then back at me. "Besides I wanted to break in this new sweater. Beau's going to wish you had your mother's knitting skills."

"Oh, Phil." My mom pokes his belly.

"About that, Dad," I begin. My lungs are primed for a sigh, but for my father's sake, I hold it in. "Beau's not going to be here this year."

"Oh, no!" His grin shifts into an exaggerated frown. For the record, Phil Graham doesn't know how to do sad very well. So his supreme effort to show me some empathy—or is it sympathy?—tugs at my heartstrings. "That's too bad, sweetie," he adds. And the lump I'd almost dislodged from my throat forms again. So I gulp it down and remind myself I need to stay strong for just a little while longer.

Beau and I made a promise to always keep the faith when it comes to one another. So I can't fail him the first holiday we're tested. And after all, the date on the calendar doesn't matter. My family already threw one weeklong Christmas in the summer. This is Christmas number two already. So Beau and I can share a third Christmas the next time he flies in to LA. That's how we've been doing things, by the way—acknowledging special events whenever we're in the same town.

First there was his birthday. Then mine. Halloween. And an early Thanksgiving. We work our celebrations around his travel schedule. Luckily, he usually has time in between assignments or at least an extended layover every few weeks. It works, but I won't pretend it isn't hard. Once I opened up the floodgates on my true feelings for Beau Slater, I couldn't shut the valve off. I feel my feelings all the time now. I'm basically a great big ball of feels.

I peek at my phone again, even though I have the sound on high, so if he texts or calls or requests a FaceChat, I won't miss it. There are no new notifications. But I haul my mouth into a smile. "We'll still make the most of this Christmas," I say. "I'm just glad to be in Abieville twice in one year. And I'm grateful Big Mama's totally well this time. And I'm especially grateful I made it before all the incoming flights got canceled."

My dad darts his eyes at my mom. "Canceled?"

My mom nods at him vigorously. "Didn't you hear? That's why Beau won't be with us. Poor thing couldn't fly into Albany. That old storm must've really kicked up last night."

My father tugs at the bottom of his Rudolf sweater. "While we were at Christmas Eve services?"

"Afterward, Phil." She frowns at him. "Obviously."

He clears his throat. "What a shame."

My mother sighs. "Betty is going to be *heartbroken*."

"Save her some fruitcake," I say, and both my parents burst out into over-the-top laughter. This makes sense when it comes to my mother. Her usual setting is way-over-the-top. But my dad is typically less ... raucous. Before I can ask if somebody spiked the eggnog, Brady appears in the hallway. His head looms above my dad. If anyone would spike a holiday beverage before noon, it would be my brother.

"What did I miss, people?" he asks, squeezing past our father through the smallish doorway. This only serves to propel Dad into the space right alongside Brady. My gaze shifts from my mom to my dad to my brother. The entire Graham family is in my bedroom now.

Normal.

"Merry Christmas, Brady." I cock an eyebrow. "Ready for your coal?"

"I never got coal."

"Which is precisely why I figured out Santa isn't real."

"Don't say that!" my mother barks, swatting my legs underneath the comforter. "Or else you'll stop feeling the magic of Christmas and the Polar Express bell won't ring for you anymore!"

I make a show of furrowing my brow. "Weren't you the one always reminding Brady and me that Christmas isn't about gifts or Santa?"

"Or snickerdoodles," Brady interjects.

Mom waves our comments away. "Of course Christmas isn't about cookies." She heaves herself off the bed. "Santa should've left stockings full of coal every year," she says.

"Now, now, Elaine," my father says. "Our kids are just spirited. We raised them to think for themselves, didn't we? And—almost as important—we wanted them to have a sense of humor." He pats his stomach, right on Rudolf's red nose. Then he wags his eyebrows at Brady and me. "You two get that from yours truly."

My mother scoffs. "Don't be ridiculous, Phil. Every funny bone in our children's bodies comes from my side of the family. The Bradfords are—"

"We know," the rest of us say in unison.

She purses her lips, but we all smile at her. After taking a beat, she smiles too. "On that note, I think I hear the oven timer."

"Christmas *is* a little bit about cinnamon rolls," Brady says. He slides his gaze over to me and drops his eyes. "Too bad Beau won't be here to enjoy them. I'm really sorry, Sis."

"How did you know that?"

"Oh." He scratches his chin and blinks. "Because he called and asked me to be extra nice to you today since he couldn't be here." Brady works his mouth into a smirk. "I told him I'd try, but *extra* nice might be a tall order."

Now there's the brother I know and love.

I throw back the comforter and find my trusty slippers waiting for me on the rug. I hate cold feet in the winter. Hopefully my dad's already got a fire roaring in the old pot-bellied stove. That's one of my favorite traditions of Christmas. It's an antique stove we inherited from Big Mama's mama. We only use it once a year. Well, twice if you count July.

"Just let me brush my teeth first," I say, shuffling behind my family into the hallway.

"I'm hungry," Brady says. "So don't do your makeup or anything. Fixing the way you look right now would take forever."

"Ha ha ha," I say. Then I look in the mirror. Yikes. Brady isn't wrong. My hair is a tumbleweed, and my eyes are hollow, so I splash some cold water on my face and whip my wild hair into a twist. A few loose strands hang down in uneven tangles. Oh well. Good enough for the people in this house.

"Hurry up, Kase!" Brady shouts from the other side of the door.

"One minute," I call out, but I take three more to brush and floss my teeth, because excellent dental hygiene is more important than cinnamon rolls. Also, I don't want to murder any of my family members with my breath. And finally, bugging Brady still gives the little girl in me a secret thrill. But the truth is we're grownups now. And Brady and I have gotten much closer these past six months. I even stopped being afraid of Natalie's intentions. Who knew they were actually all good?

As it turns out, trusting people was a thing with me for a long time. And I had decent reasons for my skepticism. But opening up to others and making myself vulnerable feels worlds better than hiding behind walls.

I peer in the mirror, hardly recognizing myself. *Who is this Kasey?* Someone who's not afraid to put her heart on the line. Someone who knows that real happiness lies in being yourself and believing you're worthy of love. *Someone who's gone as mushy as Mom's cinnamon rolls.*

I gargle with mouthwash, spit, and wipe a lingering stretch of toothpaste off my chin. All the while, my mind keeps remembering Beau won't be here today. There's a dull ache inside me, an actual physical sensation of longing to be in his arms.

If I had only one wish for Christmas, it would be to spend every day and night with that good man for the rest of my life. To that end, I've got a surprise I've been dying to share with him.

The next time we can be together, that is.

"KASEY!" Brady bangs on the door. "We're tired of waiting for you!" Bang bang bang. "Stop trying to make yourself beautiful! That's as pretty as you're gonna get!"

"COMING!" I check the mirror one last time. Welp. At least my pajamas are cute. When I throw open the door, my brother's got one fist in the air and a plate with a cinnamon roll in the other. "Awww. Thanks Brady," I say, taking the plate. I lift it to my nose and inhale the sugary sweetness.

"That one's mine," he says. So I shove half the cinnamon roll in my mouth, smearing warm frosting over half my face.

"Too late," I mumble through sticky lips.

"Too bad I already licked it," Brady says.

"Ack!" I spit the mouthful of pastry out, then bobble the plate almost dropping it. Brady swoops in to catch the plate just as someone steps around the corner.

And that's when I leap into the air and straight into the open arms of Beauregard Slater.

Chapter Eighteen

BEAU

"Ho, ho, ho," I boom at Kasey in my deepest, jolliest voice. But the last *ho* turns into an "oof" when she lands on me, squeezing the air out of my lungs. Now she's got all four limbs wrapped around me like she's a baby koala bear holding onto my fur for dear life. Of course I'm not wearing real fur. No, Kasey's got her hands full of the white trim on the Santa suit I'm in.

Actually it's Mr. Graham's suit. But since my girlfriend is planting kisses all over me now, I'm trying not to think too hard about the fact that I'm dressed like her dad. Or the fact that good old St. Nick might be the least sexy holiday mascot of all time. That's why I couldn't bring myself to velcro in the fake belly.

I've worked too hard for these abs.

When Kasey plants a final smooch on my nose and slides off onto the floor, I take a step back and take her all in. I am officially speechless. Her holiday pajamas are snow-white cotton, and hugging her curves like they were made for her. Which they definitely were because both the pajama top and the bottoms are covered in … my face.

That's right. My grinning mug is the pattern printed all over the fabric. In this particular shot, I'm wearing a backward baseball cap, and I've got a bandage stretched across my forehead. That's from the time Brady beaned me with a wild pitch and I needed stitches. But that was junior year. In high school.

I reach up and stroke the scar that's usually hidden under a wave of rumpled hair. I'm half chuckling and half breathless with surprise. "Where did you get this picture?"

"Shhh." Kasey presses a finger to her mouth. Those irresistible lips. My throat goes dry. If only I could kiss her right now without an audience of Grahams. Why is there always an audience of Grahams?

"I seriously don't remember anyone taking my picture that day."

"Didn't you get the memo?" She cocks her head. "We former yearbook editors have our secrets." Her voice is low and soft and sexy. The throaty sound of it makes my mouth even drier. When I gulp, her gaze dips from my eyes to my Adam's apple. Then to my lips.

Well, *HELLO* there, Kasey Elizabeth.

I'd start kissing her right this minute, except the rest of the Grahams still haven't made themselves scarce yet. And oh, yeah. I'm dressed like the Elf in Chief. Not romantic.

Yet.

"I missed you so much," she breathes, closing the space between us. This time she doesn't leap on me, though. So I wrap my arms around her and breathe in her sweetness.

"Me too," I say, feeling every inch of the distance that's been separating us. Luckily, we've become experts at FaceChatting until we both fall asleep. Kasey always drifts off first, despite the time difference. What can I say? I'm a night owl. And sometimes I'm also a whole day ahead of her. So her nighttime is my morning. Either way, watching Kasey Graham drool into her pillow is my new favorite thing.

That is until I can do it in a bed of our own.

"I have something for you," I say into her hair, and Kasey steps back, tipping her chin up. When our eyes lock, my heart flounders in my chest. This is it. The plan that's been in the works for the past month: Operation Christmas Surprise. Or OCS as it appeared on my text thread with Brady, in case Kasey ever saw me texting her brother about it.

I glance at him now and cough into the crook of my elbow. Not subtle. "Ahem."

Brady's eyes pop. He caught my signal to leap into action. "Oh, yeah. Yes ... All right ... Ummm ..."

Okay. My best friend isn't so much leaping into action as stammering. "Hey, Mom and Dad. I need to talk to you in the kitchen. Right away."

"Now?" Mrs. Graham protests. "But Beau just got here!"

"Yes, now." Brady frowns. Which makes his mom frown. And his dad frown. "What's this about, son?" Mr. Graham asks.

"It's about ... me borrowing money for some home renovations," Brady says. "The Kellmans said while I was renting the place, I could knock myself out. Or knock out a wall or two. So yeah. That's it. I want to bring their house into this century. I mean my house. Whatever. I just need cash, okay?"

"Now hold on a minute," Mr. Graham says. "That's exactly why we let you live here for so long after college." He shakes his head. "Lots of pennies went into your savings account instead of paying rent. I saw a statement or two come through the mail before you moved. You have plenty of money in the bank. Or at least you used to. What did you spend it all on?" He cocks an eyebrow. "Or should I say *whom*?"

"Brady has a *whom*?!" Mrs. Graham gasps. "Is that why you want to fix your house up? So you can have your *whom* over?"

"No, Mom. I don't have a whom. Or a who. Or an anyone. No girlfriend. Nobody." Why is he sputtering like that? "I just—" He widens his eyes even more. "I need to talk to you. That's all..." His voice trails off, and Kasey must catch the drift of what Brady's trying to accomplish, namely get her parents out of the room.

"Mom. Dad." She smiles at them sweetly. "Could you please just go down to the kitchen?"

Mrs. Graham pats at her Mrs. Claus hat. "But—"

"Beau hasn't tried one of your cinnamon rolls yet," she adds. And no surprise, this lights a match under Mrs. Graham.

"I'll make a fresh batch!" she yelps, grabbing Mr. Graham by the arm. "Phil, you come help me. You too, Brady. We might need more butter!"

The three of them hustle downstairs like a row of quacking ducks. They're all crazy, but I sure do love those people. Almost as much as I love this woman standing in front of me. I wait a beat, then ask Kasey to close her eyes. She lifts a brow, and exhales.

"Okay, fine. I trust you."

As I lead her to the stairs, she can't stop giggling. It's adorable. She's adorable. And she doesn't even know what's in store for her. Once we get to the living room, I tell her to open her eyes. She scrunches up her shoulders and slowly lifts her lids. Then she tilts her head, blinking at the tripod camera that's hooked up to the Grahams' television with cables.

She cuts her gaze to me. "What's going on?"

I turn around and look over my shoulder like I'm as surprised as she is. "I have no idea," I say, in an exaggerated Santa voice. "So we'd better investigate."

Kasey grabs my hand and drags me across the room. On the coffee table in front of the TV are a couple of remote controls with yellow sticky notes attached to them. The note on the left says READ ME FIRST in all caps. Kasey picks up the television remote first and reads the attached note out loud. "Turn me on," she says, with another giggle.

I puff out a laugh. "I don't think the remote means it like *that*."

"Either way." Kasey shrugs. "Kind of bossy for a post-it."

"The nerve," I agree with her, arranging my face into a mask of seriousness. "But you'd better do what the note says anyway."

Her lip curves up on one side. "Because Santa's watching?"

"Something like that."

"Fine." She clicks on the television. I've already got it programmed for the camera to stream directly onto the screen.

"There's another note," I say, nodding down at the coffee table.

Kasey scoops up the tinier remote that works with the camera. "Play me."

"Well." I splay my hands. "You heard the note." She presses play, and suddenly the television screen fills with a video.

Of Nicolas Cage.

Sitting in an armchair.

Leaning forward.

Grinning into the camera.

"Merry Christmas, Kasey," Nic Cage says, in his slow, one-of-a-kind drawl. "It's me." He smacks his knees with his hands. "Good old St. Nicolas."

"WHAT?" Kasey squawks—not unlike her mother in volume—just way cuter in every other way. Kasey pauses the video and turns to gape at me. "How on earth did you do this?"

I take the remote from her. "Just keep watching." I press play again. She cuts her gaze back to the screen, her mouth still hanging open.

"This video is only a reality thanks to your beau ..." Nicolas Cage winks. "Beau. Pun intended."

Under her breath, lips barely parted, Kasey says, "I *love* puns."

"Because I know you love puns," Nic continues.

Kasey reaches down and pinches herself. "Wait. Am I dreaming?"

"You're not dreaming, Kasey," Nic says straight into the camera. "In case you were wondering if you are. I thought you might be wondering."

Kasey stands beside me, speechless, and I watch her, mesmerized by her face. Those wide eyes. Her pink cheeks. Her wild hair in a tangle. This woman thrills me to the core. And I want to thrill her back for the rest of our lives.

"Now, before we get too deep into this," Nic Cage continues, "I've got a small confession to make. I am *not* who you think I am."

Kasey bends her neck. "I don't understand."

"What's your favorite Nicolas Cage movie?" he asks.

"National Treasure Two."

"And your second favorite?"

"FaceOff."

Nic leans back in his chair. "I *knew* that would be your answer." All these questions and responses are perfectly timed thanks to more than an hour's practice before making the final video. Kasey lets out a chuckle just as Nicolas Cage straightens in the chair. Then he reaches for his collar and starts to unbutton his crisp, white oxford shirt. Slowly. From the neck down. Eyes still glued to the screen.

Kasey starts to giggle and shake her head at the same time. "What is even *happening* right now?"

"I have no idea," I say, just as Nicolas Cage opens the top of his shirt. Scrawled across his bare torso is **PROPERTY OF KEG DO NOT TOUCH!**

"Bah!" Kasey gapes, snatching the remote back to freeze the screen. Then she sets the remote on the coffee table and moves toward the television, examining the message. "Is that ... written in Sharpie?"

I nod, even though she's facing away from me. "It appears to be."

"Wow!" She peers even closer at the screen. "Nicolas Cage is totally ripped!" Then she turns and looks back at me over her shoulder, arching an eyebrow.

"What?" I ask, feigning innocence.

"I know that's you, Beau."

"What are you talking about?"

"That's Nic Cage's head on your body. Come on, Beau! Did you really think I wouldn't recognize those smoking-hot abs?"

I press both my hands to the stomach underneath the Santa suit. "You think these abs are smoking-hot?"

"I do." She grins. "And I knew that was you from the very beginning."

I smirk. "Not from the *very* beginning."

"Okay. Maybe not at first."

"And you're not disappointed?"

"HA!" She lays a hand over her heart. "Disappointed that you made me a Nicolas Cage video for Christmas? Hardly. It's genius. And I love it. This is the best Christmas gift *ever*. But when did you turn yourself into a Nic/Beau minotaur? And how did you get your voice to sound like his?"

"A photographer never reveals his secrets."

"Deep fake video?"

"Something like that," I say.

"Well." She takes a beat and chews the edge of her lip. "I've got a surprise for you too." Her eyes start sparkling like fresh snowflakes. "I couldn't figure out a way to wrap it because mine isn't that kind of gift. But"—she hops up and down, grinning—"Mrs. Witherspoon is promoting me!"

"Already?" I let out a whoop. "Kase, that's incredible!"

"As it turns out, putting me in charge of Classifieds was just her way of making sure I was truly committed to *The Chronicle*. And I must've convinced her, because starting in the new year, I'll also be getting my own weekly column!" She finishes with a shriek of joy, and I follow that up with a long Wookie roar.

"Hey!" She laughs. "I'm Chewie. You're Han."

I move in for a hug, then pick her up and spin her around the room until we're both breathless and dizzy.

"This is all incredible news," I gasp, setting her back down, "but I'm not surprised your boss sees the same potential in you as I do. You've earned this, Kasey."

"There's more," she says, and her whole face is glowing. "My column is going to be about young twenty-somethings traveling the world." She cocks an eyebrow. "Which means I'll be able to go on shoots with you." My heart skips a beat. How did I get so lucky? Kasey lifts a finger. "Not all of them, of course. Just the ones that make sense for my job."

"I'll take it," I blurt out.

Kasey points at me. "I'll take YOU!"

"Perfect." I grin. "So now you should really watch the rest of your video."

"Huh?"

I nod at the frozen screen. "It wasn't over." I pick up the remote and press play. Kasey's focus shifts back to the video as Nic bends down and pulls up a handmade sign. In Sharpie, of course. Her eyes go wide when she reads the message.

CHECK YOUR STOCKING.

"Ha!" She claps her hands, skipping over to the fireplace like a kid on Christmas. Then she slides the stocking with her name off the hook on the mantle. Before she digs inside, she pauses.

"Go on," I prompt.

She wrinkles her nose. "What if there's a mousetrap in there?"

I chuckle. "There's not a mousetrap."

Still her hand trembles as she reaches in and pulls out a red velvet pouch from Murphy's jewelers. She swallows hard. "What is this?"

I shrug. "Only one way to find out."

She unties the small pouch, flips it over and blinks at what drops into her hand. "It's a snowman," she whispers, staring at the tiny charm cradled in her palm.

"For your bracelet. To symbolize our first Christmas as a real couple."

She gulps again and nods, then she turns to me, her eyes welling up. "It's absolutely perfect."

Her cheeks flush pink, and she comes toward me, shoving the sleeves of her Beau Slater pajamas up her arm. Then she lifts her wrist and hands me the charm. "Will you do the honors?"

I gently turn her wrist over and release the clasp to add the new charm to the rest. And as I clip the bracelet back on, my whole body floods with warmth. From the softness of her skin. The shine in her eyes. The bright future ahead.

For us.

"I love it, Beau. I love *you*. Thank you so much." When she moves in to kiss me, I glance over her shoulder out the bay window.

"What if I told you there's more where that came from?"

"I don't need anything else," she says. "You and Nicolas Cage's hot abs and this snowman charm are all I want for Christmas." When I reach for her hand, she tilts her head.

"Trust me," I say. Then I lead her to the entryway. There's a pair of boots and a jacket on a bench that Brady planted for me earlier. While Kasey tugs on the boots and jacket, my pulse starts to race. I wait for her to stand and, with a flourish, I pull the door open wide.

There, in the middle of the Graham's walkway, is a freshly-built snowman. But this is a real one.

He's got on a top hat and a carrot for a nose. Three Oreo cookies act as buttons. His arms are two sticks with a silver tray balanced across them. In the center is a small velvet box.

"Beau!" Kasey squeaks. "*That* is not a charm." Her knees start to buckle, and I wrap an arm around her waist.

"Don't quit on me now, Kasey Graham. Let's go say hi to Frosty." As we trudge across the yard, I gulp, trying to act cool, but my heart is banging against my ribs. When we reach the snowman, I pick up the box and drop to a knee.

If the snow is cold, I can't tell.

"Ohhhhh." Kasey sucks in a breath, and I gaze up at her.

"I know this might seem fast," I say quickly, "but I can't wait any longer." My voice catches, and Kasey exhales. It's like we're in sync, breathing for each other. "I can't believe I waited this long in the first place," I continue, and she nods at me, lids fluttering. "I waited all morning. And six months before that." My heart pounds inside my chest. "The truth is I've been waiting my whole life for this moment. Everything between us has all been leading up to ... this."

I pop open the box with a soft snap, and inside is the ring: a perfect solitaire with sapphire baguettes on either side.

"Beau," Kasey says on a gasp.

"The two smaller stones are for our past and our present," I tell her.

"They're beautiful." She sniffles, her eyes bright.

"Those sapphires are just drops in the bucket compared to the diamond that represents what I want for us."

"What do you want?" she asks.

"Forever," I say. "With you."

A bright tear rolls down Kasey's cheek, and I almost leap to my feet so I can kiss it, but I have to ask the question first. And if she answers yes, I'll be there for every other drop of joy life brings us. For the rest of our lives.

"Kasey Elizabeth Graham, will you make me the happiest man on earth and be my wife, while I travel this world as your devoted husband?"

Another tear dribbles down the other side of her face, and she sniffles and nods and blurts out, "Yes. Yes. YES! I'm dying to marry you, Beau Slater!"

I leap to my feet and wrap my arms around Kasey, who buries her face in the neck of the suit. It's possible dressing as Santa was a miss. But the woman I love said yes to me anyway, so I wouldn't change a single thing about today.

"Your proposal was perfect," Kasey says, tipping her face up to mine. "Better than anything I could've come up with. And I'm the writer in the family." Then she goes up on her toes and presses her lips to mine. They're soft and sweet and wet with tears. Happy tears.

The happiest tears.

Off to the side, the front door creaks. Kasey and I turn as the door opens slowly. Mrs. Graham peeks her head out first, testing the waters. Then she waves the rest of the family out onto the porch. Brady converges on me first, clapping me on the back.

"Welcome to the family," he announces. "You know I always wanted a brother." He turns to Kasey. "No offense."

"None taken," she says. She spins around and looks at her parents. "Did you have any idea Beau was going to do this today?"

"Of course!" Mrs. Graham crows at the exact same time Mr. Graham shakes his head and says, "Not a clue."

Mrs. Graham humphs. "Maybe *you* were clueless, Phil," she says. "But nothing gets past me."

Kasey's father shrugs. "Beau did speak to us back in July before he started visiting you in LA. So I suppose we did see this coming. Just not exactly when. Or what Beau would be wearing."

"The suit was my idea," Brady says. "I thought maybe Kasey could sit on Santa's lap."

"Uh, yeah no," I chime in. "That was *not* part of the plan."

"Speaking of which." Kasey gathers my hand in hers. "Let's get you out of this costume and into your brand new Christmas pajamas." Her mouth quirks. "I'll give you one guess what's on them."

"Oh, man." I chuckle. "I hope it's *your* face and not Brady's."

Kasey gives my fingers a squeeze. "Hope springs eternal."

I look down at her ring. "It certainly does."

Epilogue

ONE YEAR LATER

KASEY

I smile down at Natalie and Brady, who are sitting next to one another on my parents' old sofa. I'm standing above them, practically vibrating with excitement. More to the point, I am literally vibrating. That's because Beau's been blowing up my phone all morning. He's back in LA, waiting for me. I'm still in Abieville, ready to head to the airport in an hour. I slip the phone from the pocket of my sweatshirt and check his latest message.

Beau: Did you ask her yet?
Me: I will as soon as you stop texting me (heart eyes)

Shoving my phone back in my pocket, I clear my throat and smile. "We are gathered here today—"

"Excuse me," Brady breaks in, wearing a frown. I can't tell if he's confused or annoyed, but neither is the vibe I'm going for. "Why do you sound like you're officiating a wedding?" he asks.

"This *is* about the wedding," I say. "If you'd just let me continue—"

"Yeah, Brady," Natalie says. She faces him and shrugs. "Stop interrupting, and let your sister talk."

He gives Nat some serious side-eye. "You just interrupted her too."

They both cross their arms over their chests.

What is up with these two today?

Actually, to be honest, Brady's been acting kind of strange for a while now. But I've got less than an hour before I leave for the airport, and I'm way too excited to let my brother bring me down.

"I'm going to start over," I say. "Because I have a whole speech prepared, and you two kind of messed me up."

"We're so sorry," Nat chirps brightly. But Brady just harrumphs.

"Okay." I take a deep breath. I've got to get this done before my flight. And also before Beau texts me again, which could be any minute at the rate he's going. "We are gathered here today because Beau and I are getting married this summer—as you are both already aware—and Brady is going to be Beau's best man."

"Let me guess." Brady sighs. "You're finally asking Nat to be a bridesmaid."

"Shhh!" Natalie lays a hand over Brady's mouth. Instead of backing away, he turns and stares Nat down. They stay frozen for several moments—eyes locked—his lips blocked by her palm.

"Ahem." I clear my throat, and Natalie lowers her hand, still looking at Brady.

"If your sister is going to ask me to be in her wedding party," she says to him, "I'd like *her* to do it."

"But I'm *not* asking you to be a bridesmaid," I say. Nat cuts her eyes to me, and Brady scoffs. "Awkward," he says out of one corner of his mouth.

Natalie thumps his shoulder. "YOU'RE awkward."

"Hold on a minute," I say. "This isn't awkward. It's not awkward at all. This is the opposite of awkward! In fact, it's totally awesome." I wait for them to shift their focus back to me and beam at them both. "You see, I don't have a sister. And yes, of course I adore all my cousins, but I could never pick just one of them to be—"

"Oooohhh!" Natalie's blue eyes widen.

"—my maid of honor."

"YES, YES, YES!" Nat leaps up from the couch and pounces on me so quickly, I'm surprised we don't crash backward over the coffee table. She hugs me hard while jumping up and down, and I end up having to spit out a mouthful of her hair. When Natalie finally lets go, her whole face is shining. "Do you really want *me*?" she asks.

"I do."

From the couch, Brady huffs out a breath. "Still sounds like a wedding."

Natalie ignores him, keeping her eyes on me. "And Beau's not making you do this?" she asks.

I shake my head. "Nope."

"And my mom didn't try to talk you into it?"

"No."

"Or your mom, either?"

"Nah." I shrug. "My mom can't make me do anything I don't want to do."

"Heh." Brady smirks. "I can't believe you said that with a straight face." He rises from the couch slowly, with an exaggerated stretch and groan.

"Seriously, Brady." I wrinkle my nose. "Why are you being such a grump?"

"Because I still don't get why I had to be around for this," he says. "Natalie's going to be your maid of honor, and that's truly, *truly* fantastic." He splays his hands, but it's like his fingers have been dipped in sarcasm. "The thing is Beau asked me to be his best man months ago. So. Why am I here now?"

"I'm about to explain," I say, pointing at the couch. "Sit. Both of you." Natalie backs up first, landing in her original seat. When Brady drops down next to her, he's so close, their legs bump. She nudges him, and he frowns. Then he readjusts with a grunt.

"So Beau and I have this idea we think could be really cool, but it will mean a little more work on your ends."

"Perfect," Brady groans. "Just what I need. Even more work to worry about."

"Wait." A tiny alarm bell sounds in my head, and I drop my arms. "Is something wrong at the clinic?"

Brady cuts his gaze away from me and swipes a hand down his face like he's trying to erase all traces of emotion. "Nothing. It's fine. Sorry to be a jerk. What were you saying, Kasey?"

I tilt my head and study his expression. There's definitely more to this story, but I know from experience that if Brady's not ready to share, he won't.

"So what's the idea?" Natalie asks, bringing us back around to my subject.

Brady's hands are tense now, resting on his kneecaps. "Yeah. Seriously. What can we do for you guys?"

I nod, forging forward. "Beau and I decided we want to get married here in Abieville. More specifically, we're planning a July ceremony at the lake. On the beach. At sunset."

"That sounds amazing," Natalie gushes.

"She already asked you to be maid of honor," Brady mumbles.

"Anyway," I continue, "our wedding party lives all over the globe—and everyone probably can't meet up together until the week of the wedding. So." I grin. "To make things interesting, I'm going to give each of my bridesmaids—"

"—and your maid of honor?" Natalie chimes in.

"Right. I'm going to give each of my bridesmaids *and* my maid of honor four yards of raw silk and have you make your own dresses. That way you can each tailor your designs to your personal style, but you'll all have the same fabric. The look will be cohesive, but you'll still be individuals. It's a way to match without being ... you know ... matchy-matchy."

"I LOVE IT!" Natalie shrieks.

"Oh, yay!" I exhale with relief. I can't wait to marry Beau, but I also want everyone else to be happy with their roles in our wedding. "You really don't mind having to find a design and a seamstress?"

"Not at all!"

Brady arches an eyebrow. "Don't tell me. Beau's giving his groomsmen four yards of raw silk to make our own tuxedos?"

"Ha ha, Brady." I shake my head. "Obviously not. But he *does* want you all to pick out your own Hawaiian shirts for a luau-themed bachelor party."

"Whoa." Natalie crinkles her nose. "My brother wants a bachelor party? I'm kind of surprised."

"He's having it at The Beachfront Inn," I tell her. "We heard the last couple years have been rough on their business, so we figured a bachelor party would be a good excuse to spend some extra money there. We can have a bachelorette party, too. On the same night."

"In separate rooms," Brady adds.

"That figures." Natalie huffs out a breath. "You wouldn't want to get too close to all our irresistible lady-ness. Who *knows* what might happen?"

"Irresistible lady-ness?"

"It's a thing."

Brady guffaws. "Most of the bridesmaids are my cousins." He takes a beat, and his mouth slips sideways. "But don't worry, Nat. I promise I can control myself around the ones who aren't."

"I wasn't worried," Natalie quips.

"Good."

"GOOD!"

"Do I have to send you both to your room for a time out?"

They both look at me, jaws slack.

"I was kidding," I say slowly. "And I have no idea why you're both being so weird, but let me remind you it was your idea to push Beau and me together in the first place. So get over yourselves and get onboard with this. For my whole life, I'll only have one brother and one sister-in-law," I say.

"Well." Natalie's forehead creases.

"What?"

"When Brady gets married someday, you'll have *two* sisters-in-law." She blinks, like she's considering the math. "But I'll probably be better than whoever *she* is."

"I'm sure you're right," I say. Then I lift a finger. "So adjusted statistics: I'll only ever have *one* brother and two sisters-in-law at the most. Either way, this wedding will be the happiest day of my life, with all my favorite people on the planet." Even as the words come out, I feel the truth of them in my bones. And my heart skips a beat.

"Happiest day." Natalie lays a palm over her heart and sighs. "I like the sound of that. And we'll be there for you and Beau. All the way." She elbows my brother. "Right, Brady?" When he doesn't reply, she elbows him again, harder. "Won't we be there for Beau and Kasey, no matter what?" As Natalie says this, she's still got her eyes glued to mine.

Brady is focused on me too. "I will," he mutters.

I puff out a laugh. "*Now* who sounds like he's at a wedding?" Before Brady can retort, my phone vibrates in the pocket of my sweatshirt. I slide it out and see another text from my super-hot future husband, whose gorgeous face is melting my lock screen.

Beau: ???!!!

I grin at Natalie. "It's your brother again. He keeps checking every five minutes to see if I've asked you yet. He's so excited for you to be in the wedding party."

She hops up from the couch. "I'll go call him now."

"In the meantime," I say, "I'd better go get my bags. Mom and Dad will be back from The Shop any minute to take me to the airport."

As I climb the stairs to my bedroom, I'm feeling light as a feather. No, lighter than *air*. I'm engaged to my soulmate, and I've just asked his sister to be my maid of honor. Everything is working out better than I ever could've dreamed. I grab my suitcase and sling my carryon over my shoulder. Then I bump back down the stairs and into the empty living room.

Huh.

Nat's probably out on the porch calling Beau now, and I can hear someone moving around in the kitchen. I'll bet it's Brady raiding the pantry. He always comes by to steal food from Mom and Dad, and I can't blame him. I'd do the same if I lived as close to them as he does.

As long as my parents aren't back from the store yet, and I've got Brady here alone, I can ask him what he meant about working so hard *for no reason*.

So I set my carryon on the sofa and leave my suitcase by the door. Then I head straight to the kitchen. Rounding the corner, I come upon Brady. And Natalie. And they're kissing.

KISSING?!

Wait. They *can't* be kissing.

Can they?

When I gasp, Natalie squeaks and shoves Brady away so hard, he pinwheels backward into the refrigerator. "Ouch!" he yelps, rubbing the back of his head.

"We were just baking brownies!" Nat blurts.

I stand there, gaping at both of them. "Baking brownies?" I manage to choke out. "Is that what the kids call it these days?"

Natalie's not making eye contact with me, but she *is* turning crimson from forehead to throat. "Brady was just checking to see ... if you have ... enough ... umm ..."

"Butter," he says, squaring his shoulders. "I was just checking to see if we had enough ... butter." He turns and opens the fridge, then starts digging around inside.

I shift my weight, suddenly embarrassed. But why should I be embarrassed? They're the ones who were just caught with their hands in the proverbial cookie jar. I arch an eyebrow. "How much butter do you need to make brownies?"

"A lot," Natalie rushes to say. "I think. A *very* lot."

"A very lot of butter," I repeat. "Got it."

Brady pulls open the crisper, then slams it shut again. "Too bad we're totally out. No butter whatsoever."

"Are you sure?" I ask. "Not even a *little* lot?"

And that's when the door from the side yard into the kitchen flies open with a bang. My mother bustles in with two big bags of groceries. My father follows close behind with two more bags.

"Look who we ran into at The Shop," Mom warbles just as Betty and Dale Slater come through the door.

"Well, I hope you bought some butter *and* popcorn," I say. "Because this show is starting to get interesting..."

***

Order *That Time I Kissed The Groomsman Grump* now to find out what happens with Natalie and Brady! And sign up for my newsletter to receive *His Third Second Chance* free!

Acknowledgments

I feel like I get worse at these with every book (which is unfortunate, since I have more gratitude than ever) but I'll still give it a shot, knowing I've got more people to thank than I have breath in my body.

So I'll start with my incredible ARC team. I approached you all last-minute during one of the busiest reading months of the year, and you graciously squeezed this book into your schedules. Y'all are incredible, and I am beyond fortunate to have you in my corner.

Jo, Ranee, and Kaylee, you are the best kind of support system. Thank you for always sticking by me, no matter how messy the manuscripts might be when I send them to you.

Shaela, my brilliant cover designer, I adore you and your patience. Thank you so much for everything you've continued to do for my books and me.

All my author friends (you know who you are) I am lifted up by you daily. Encouraged. Inspired. Transformed. Knowing someone else understands this exact rollercoaster we're on is a genuine lifesaver. Plus you are even more hilarious in real life than you are in your books. And that's saying something!

To every person who has chosen one or more of my stories to fit into their precious reading time, you are a dream come true. Honestly. For my entire life, I wanted to be an author, and you make this real for me over and over and over.

To my doggie pals, thank you for keeping me company,

keeping me humble, and being fodder for my Instagram reels. (You're the cutest three rescue pups in the history of canines.)

And to Bill, Jack, and Karly — as ever — you are my life. Forever.

The end.

Also by Julie Christianson

The Apple Valley Love Stories Series:

The Mostly Real McCoy: A Sweet Romantic Comedy (Apple Valley Love Stories Book 1)

My Own Best Enemy: A Sweet Romantic Comedy (Apple Valley Love Stories Book 2)

Pretending I Love Lucy: A Sweet Romantic Comedy (Apple Valley Love Stories Book 3)

The Even Odder Couple: A Sweet Romantic Comedy (Apple Valley Love Stories Book 4)

The Time of Your Life Series

That Time I Kissed My Brother's Best Friend

That Time I Kissed The Groomsman Grump

Free Bonus Story

His Third Second Chance

About the Author

Julie Christianson writes sweet romantic comedies—that is when she's not reading them. A former English teacher and lapsed marathon runner, Julie lives in Southern California with her one husband, two kids, and three dogs. She's madly in love with all of them, but there's not a lot of room on her couch.

To learn more, visit her website, and follow her on Amazon, BookBub, and Instagram!